CRAZY VANILLA

Everything seems to be going wrong for Tyler Woodruff. His father barely acknowledges his existence, his mother is drinking more than is good for her and his brother, Cameron, has been banished from the family for announcing that he is gay. When, to cap it all, Tyler discovers that his passion for wildlife photography is leading him heavily into debt, he decides that the only way to remain solvent is to win the one thousand dollar prize offered by his local ice-cream parlour for the best name for a new ice-cream. Arriving at the ice-cream parlour too late for the prize-giving ceremony — and discovering that he hasn't won, anyway — Tyler meets Mitzi Gerrard, and from then on, things take a distinct turn for the better.

ALSO BY BARBARA WERSBA

Tunes for a Small Harmonica

CRAZY VANILLA

BARBARA WERSBA

THE BODLEY HEAD
LONDON

The author gratefully acknowledges permission to
reprint the following: 'Not Waving but Drowning'
from Stevie Smith, *Collected Poems*. Copyright © 1972
by Stevie Smith. Reprinted by permission of New
Directions Publishing Corporation.
Quotation from *The Outermost House* by Henry
Beston, copyright © 1928, 1949, copyright © 1956 by
Henry Beston, copyright © by Elizabeth C. Beston.
Reprinted by permission of Henry Holt & Company.

This novel was first published in New York and this
British edition was produced by photographing the
American text. To have altered the American spelling
would have greatly added to the expense of
production and would have meant increasing the
published price of the book, so the American spelling
and vocabulary have been retained throughout.

British Library Cataloguing in Publication Data
Wersba, Barbara
Crazy Vanilla.
I. Title
813'.54[J] PZ7
ISBN 0-370-31056-X

ONE

There is a place on the end of Long Island, in New York, that is called The Hamptons—and I suppose you could describe this place as a lot of little towns strung together near the ocean. Another way of describing it would be as one big cocktail party surrounded by water, because The Hamptons is a very social environment. Especially in summer. Woody Allen comes down here, and Lauren Bacall, and Truman Capote had a house here for a long time before he died—and then there are the rest of us. The towns have names like Southampton, and East Hampton, and Water Mill and Sag Harbor, and some of the houses are very elaborate. One of my big entertainments used

1

to be reading the "summer rentals" column in the local paper every spring. The houses along the ocean would be advertised for ten and twenty thousand dollars a month—that's right, a month—yet nobody thought this was strange.

I don't know why I'm talking about money when I really want to talk about a person named Mitzi Gerrard, but somehow it seems relevant. We're not poor—in the sense that my father is a broker on Wall Street, and my grandfather was a banker, and my mother's family were in textiles down South. For as long as I can remember, we've had a place in The Hamptons (North Haven) and a New York apartment, and a house in Florida.

Which is why the whole thing of my photography became such an issue. I mean, my father could have afforded to get me the stuff I needed, the equipment and so forth, but he absolutely refused—and since I could not get all this equipment on my allowance, I went to work. Not that working after school and in the summers is so bad, but I was only in the seventh grade when I started.

It was all because my father had discovered that my brother Cameron is gay. He opened a love letter to Cameron written by someone named David, and hit the ceiling. I was twelve at the time, and Cameron was nineteen and still living at home. Well, my father read this letter by accident and fell apart. My mother (who drinks a bit too much) headed for the vodka, and my father and Cameron had a violent discussion about AIDS. Not that this was a real issue—because Cameron had been in the closet up till that time, and had never been promiscuous.

But the point is, my father had just discovered that Cameron was gay when I told him that I wanted to be a photographer. We were sitting in the library of our North Haven house when I told him this. He looked at me oddly.

"A photographer? I'm not sure I understand you, Tyler."

"Well," I said, "I just want to take pictures for the rest of my life. That's all."

"You want to become a professional photographer?"

"Yes, sir. I do."

My father thought about this for a moment. "Journalism?" he said. "News photography?"

"Well, no. Not exactly."

"Portrait photography?"

"No, sir," I said. "Birds."

And that's when my father—who is in his fifties and has a terrible temper—lost his mind. *"What?"* he said. "What did you say?"

"Birds," I said in a small voice. "Wildlife."

"I don't understand you, Tyler."

3

"Herons," I said in an even smaller voice. "Swans. I want to photograph swans."

I have to reiterate the point that my father might not have lost his mind that day if he hadn't just learned about Cameron. I mean, *in no way* is there anything effeminate about photographing birds. Think of the great nature photographers like Ansel Adams and Eliot Porter and people like that. But for some reason, my father decided that becoming a bird photographer was sissy.

"I will not contribute a penny to this!" he said. "If you want to photograph swans, you will do it on your own time. As a hobby. Meanwhile, you will continue to maintain an A-average in school. Is that understood?"

I forgot to mention that my father expects me to go to Harvard. I have also forgotten to mention that I am supposed to study finance and become a banker like my grandfather. Cameron was supposed to go to Harvard too, to study law, but he refused and became an interior designer.

All of which is why I became an underground photographer at the age of twelve. Wildlife photography is not easy to do in New York City, but there was always Central Park and the Bronx Zoo, and places like that. Then a stroke of luck happened. My mother decided to live in the North Haven house year-round, with my father coming

4

down weekends, and by this time Cameron had moved out of the apartment completely. That left me—and I opted to live with Mother, in The Hamptons, where the bird life is fantastic. It meant that I had to go to Southampton Country-Day, which is a stupid and snobbish school, but I didn't care. All I wanted was to keep working on my photography.

I want to say a few words now about Cameron, because he is so important to this story. To begin with, Cameron is very good-looking, with pale blond hair and bright blue eyes, and he is terrifically talented. The best swimmer, the best bridge player, the best everything. But beyond the fact that he is so gifted and good-looking is the fact that he is a caring person. Cameron has always cared about me as much as he cares about himself, and when I was little he would devote hours and hours to me. Helping me with my homework, teaching me how to swim and play tennis. Things like that. And when I started photography two years ago (I'm fourteen now) he was the only person who understood. I didn't dare show my pictures to Father, but when Cameron saw my first successful one—a photo of a great white egret taking off from a marsh—he flipped. "It's tremendous," he said. "You're an artist, Tyler, a natural." Well, no one had ever called me an artist before, and I was very moved. But I have to admit that it's a good picture. The egret has just taken off from the water, and its long neck is thrust forward and its wings are uplifted. The background is a blurred bottle-green and the bird's feet have made a silver splash.

From that day on I showed all of my pictures to Cameron. Cameron is a very visual person, which is probably why he went into interior design, and his criticisms are excellent. He bought me some books on photography, and a tripod, and was tremendously helpful. I guess I had always admired Cameron more than I realized—loved him more than I realized—because when he was forced to explain to me about being gay I was stunned.

I pretended not to be, of course. I mean, I would support Cameron in anything he did. But this was different. He was talking about his sex life, about liking men, and it shook me up.

Father had opened the letter from David that evening, along with a pile of his own mail, because the handwriting on the envelope looked like his lawyer's handwriting. But after he realized what the letter was, there had been an explosion in front of everyone—me, Mother, Cameron, our maid Agnes—and then Father had stormed out of the house. Mother poured herself a double vodka and retreated to the den (this was in the New York apartment), which left Cameron and me alone in the living room. Cameron had gone pale, absolutely white, and for a long time he couldn't look at me. Finally, he said, "I'm sorry you had to hear all that, Tyler."

I shrugged and pretended to be very calm, which I wasn't. "It doesn't matter."

"But it does matter, old buddy. I can see that you're shocked."

Well, hell, I was only twelve. So of course I was shocked. "It's OK," I said to him.

Cameron, who never drinks hard liquor, poured himself a glass of scotch and sat down on the couch. "I think we should talk."

I sat down in an armchair across the room. After a moment, I said, "Have you always been gay?"

He looked me squarely in the eye. "Always."

"How come?" I asked.

"I don't know. Just born that way, I guess."

"Couldn't you change? I mean, to please Father."

To my amazement, he laughed. "Tyler, people can't change such things. We are what we are."

"But Father was furious."

"He'll get over it. Or maybe he won't. I don't give a damn, either way."

I went over and sat next to him on the couch. "I'd like to understand," I said. And it was the truth.

He put his arm around my shoulders. "OK, Tyler. I've known I was gay since I was your age, around eleven or twelve, but since nobody in this world wants to be different, I practiced denial. Tried to like girls, to date a lot, to be an average guy. But I'm not an average guy, I'm me—and if I don't face this now, I'm going to suffer later on. I mean, I don't want to be one of those fellows who marries and then sees men on the side. I want to be honest with my life, even if Father disinherits me. It sounds corny, but Shakespeare was right—if you're true to yourself, then you can't be false to anyone else. I just hope this doesn't come between you and me. Because you matter a lot."

"Is there a chance that you could get that disease?" I asked. "You know what I mean."

"There's a chance of anything," he said. "Life is hazardous."

I knew then that I was out of my depth, and that what I didn't understand about this subject would fill an encyclopedia. I also knew—and it was an eerie feeling—that Cameron had a secret life I had never suspected.

"Is it immoral to be gay?" I asked him.

"No. It isn't."

"People say it is."

"People are wrong."

"Are animals ever gay?"

He grinned. "Sure. Quite often."

For some reason, the fact that there were gay animals in the world made me feel better. I had a sudden image of gay raccoons and foxes playing in the woods—of gay otters swimming cheerfully on their backs in Scottish lakes. I looked at my brother. "I don't really understand all this. But I love you, Cameron."

Suddenly there were tears in his eyes. "I love you too," he said. "You're the best."

The next day I went off to a bookstore on Fifth Avenue and bought six paperbacks on the subject of homosexuality. I had been a little nervous about purchasing these books, but the clerk didn't even blink an eye when he took my money. And the minute I got home, I locked myself in my room and read parts of all six books. They weren't helpful because, first of all, none of the authors agreed with one another about what homosexuality *was*, and secondly because the stuff about sex in these books was too graphic for me. This kind of material doesn't bother me now, but in those days it disturbed me. So for a while there was a secret pain inside me whenever Cameron and I were together. I couldn't have told anyone, but in some strange way I was suffering.

Father was too. Except that his way of showing it was anger. And he and Cameron had so many arguments about AIDS—behind closed doors—that eventually Cameron couldn't stand it, and left home. Father is very tight with money, and for that reason Cameron had never been able to afford his own apartment. But one night after they had had a violent argument, Cameron walked out, without taking his clothes or his books or anything. He was in his last year at the Institute of Design, where he had gone after bumming around Europe for a while, but outside of the school's address on 57th Street, we didn't know where he was.

I haven't said anything about Mother yet, but she took Cameron's departure very hard. She adores Cameron, and I don't think she had moral objections about him being gay. But since she is slightly afraid of Father, her remarks were muted. She did the same thing I did, however, which was to buy all these books on homosexuality and read them on the sly. Whether they were of any help to her, I don't know.

Mother comes from Birmingham, Alabama, and was a debutante down there and had a big coming-out party when she was eighteen. Marrying her was probably the only frivolous thing Father ever did. Because, as you may have guessed by now, Father is a somber person. Mother, on the other hand, is blond and vivacious and a little on the plump side—a person who loves sociability, but who has a rather bad drinking problem. This has been very painful to us, because she tends to talk too loud at cocktail parties, and flirt with other people's husbands, and then the next morning she is depressed. They are an odd couple—Father who rarely smiles, and Mother who always wants to keep up a good front, and who calls people "honey" or "sugar" much of the time.

There are times when I have come upon Mother sitting at the kitchen table with a drink in her hand, when I realize that she is not the person she pretends to be. At these moments, without her makeup or her hair done, she looks very grim, and you can tell that her main relationship is not with people but with alcohol. Alcohol is her buddy, her best friend, and it depresses me very much. If I hadn't met Mitzi Gerrard last summer, I would probably be in therapy by now. But Mitzi changed everything, and that's what this story is about.

TWO

I want to take a few moments here to explain how I got into photography, because it's pertinent to everything that happened later on. Someone had given me an Instamatic camera for Christmas, one of my cousins actually, and so I started fooling around with it. As I have said earlier, I was twelve at the time. Well, there was a pigeon living on the window ledge outside my room, in the New York apartment, and the more I watched this pigeon, the more I realized that it was not entirely well. It just sat on the window ledge with its eyes closed—and every so often it would make a little noise, not a cooing noise, but something harsher. I had this terrible feeling that it was going to die, but I also knew that it was a good subject for the camera. So I started photographing it. All in all, I took one hundred and eight pictures of that pigeon, and out of the group there was one picture that actually moved me, because it had captured the essence of a sick pigeon so perfectly. I had put birdseed on the ledge for the pigeon, and an ashtray with water in it, but the bird never touched these things, and one day it was gone. But I knew I was on to something important, and so I took my savings out of the bank and bought a better camera, and began to work in color.

First it was just the birds in Central Park, the warblers, finches, orioles, and so forth. Next it was the more exotic birds at the Bronx Zoo. *Then* I learned that North Haven is a paradise for birds, especially in the fall and the spring. The eastern end of Long Island is situated on the Atlantic Flyway, which is a kind of bird superhighway in the sky, and when I realized that at my very fingertips were egrets and herons and Canada geese, and mute swans, I got very excited. It never occurred to me to wonder why I should suddenly love birds instead of cats or dogs, or horses. I just clicked with birds, and they with me, and the subject became an obsession.

I began to divide the year into phases that were connected with birds. In The Hamptons, spring meant great white egrets and snowy egrets and least bitterns. Fall meant blue herons. Winter, especially January and February, meant swans—my favorite bird—because that's when swans have their battles over territory and do these fantastic mating dances. July and August are very quiet months in the bird world. The young are being raised, or already have been raised, and the birds in The Hamptons have retreated because of all the goddam summer people. But occasionally, at the bay beach, you will see a group of swans flying over, and this is very thrilling. One of the best pictures I have ever taken is of two swans flying low over the water. Their necks are thrust forward, and their wings are beating like crazy, and there is a terrific feeling of motion in the picture. I sent this picture away to the *Wildlife International* magazine photo contest, and while it didn't win a prize they wrote me a very good letter about it.

Most people are indifferent to bird photography. But you might want to know that I use a 35mm SLR camera (a Canon) and that I work exclusively in color. I don't do my own developing yet, because color developing demands a lot of equipment, so the developing is done by the Speedy-Print Photo Shop in Sag Harbor, which is just over the bridge from our house. At first I thought it was a cop-out to use the camera on automatic, but then I realized that there is simply *no time* to do manual settings when you are photographing birds. The moment is over in a moment, if you understand what I mean, and you have to be quick. You also have to know a lot about the birds' habits and habitats. Last spring I finally located a swan on a nest, which is something I've been trying to do for years. The nest was on a little island, in the middle of a pond, and the day that my binoculars picked this up a chill went down my spine. The nest was very high, to avoid flooding, and the female swan was sleeping on top of it with her neck folded back between her wings. The male swan was circling the island like a sentinel, very alert, very fierce. My heart began to pound, and I ripped the lens cap off my Canon T-50 and started to focus my zoom lens.

Then, for the thousandth time, I realized that my 80–200 zoom just wouldn't do it. I needed a longer lens, an 85–300 probably, and my frustration was so terrible that I just sat down on the ground and gave up. This was my main problem. To photograph birds that were at a distance, I needed a lens that cost five hundred and forty dollars.

How does a fourteen-year-old person acquire five hundred and forty dollars? I couldn't walk into the local bank and apply for a loan because

I was too young. And no matter how many lawns I mowed during the summer, and how many swimming pools I painted, five hundred was still a lot to accumulate. There was something ridiculous about the situation, because Father is not exactly poor—but I knew if I asked him for five hundred dollars he would faint. To understand Father, you have to realize that he drives a Mercedes that is so old that it is considered a classic. Collectors offer him money for this vehicle all the time, because it is so ancient, but he refuses to buy anything newer because the car still runs. Then there is the North Haven house, which was once a carriage house, and which is so cold in the winters that Mother and I have to wear long underwear under our clothes. The ceilings in this house are two stories high, there is no insulation, and the pipes freeze every January because Father insists that we keep the thermostat down.

Seeing that swan on its nest, and realizing once again that my lens was not long enough to photograph it, made me feel crazy. I felt bitter against the whole world, and wondered how I would ever get the pictures I wanted. I thought of becoming a jewel thief, of robbing a cash register at the Mighty King Supermarket. Then it hit me. I would enter Olsen's Annual Ice-Cream-Naming Contest. The prize money was one thousand dollars.

A word of explanation is needed here to explain that Olsen's is a very elegant ice-cream parlor in Sag Harbor, and that every spring Mr. Olsen holds a contest in which people invent the name of a new ice cream. One year the winner was Riotous Raspberry. Another year it was Peerless Pistachio. All I had to do was come up with a good name for a new ice cream—which Mr. Olsen would create a recipe for—and win the prize.

I was still sitting on the cold ground watching that swan (it was early April) but my mind was on ice cream. Marvelous Mocha? Banana Bulge? No good. It had to be something brilliant. Because that 85–300 Canon zoom was almost within my reach. I saw myself taking the bus to some very good camera store and handing over five hundred and forty dollars for my lens. I saw myself—someday—winning the *Wildlife International* nature photography contest.

Seductive Strawberry? I said to myself, as I walked home that day. Amazing Almond? Not good enough, not good enough. What I needed was an ice cream that sounded like nothing else in the world.

THREE

There are a few things I haven't mentioned yet, and one of them is that my last name is Woodruff. Woodruff is not a bad name, but Tyler Woodruff has always sounded affected to me. Not that people at Southampton Country-Day don't have affected names. Some of the girls have names like Blair and Sydney, and there is a boy in my class called Maxwell. He wants to be a professional boxer.

I'm writing this in January, which means that I've been a freshman in the upper school for four months now. But out of the entire freshman class, I haven't made one friend. Every single person in the upper school thinks I'm crazy—and all because of the bird pictures.

It was the same way in the eighth grade. A boy in my class named George McIver told me that his uncle was a Time-Life photographer, so I figured that George might have an eye for pictures and brought my one good egret photo to school. McIver looked at it oddly. "This is what you photograph?" he asked me. "Birds?" "Well, yes," I said. "Sure." But I could see that the idea of anyone photographing birds turned McIver off. As luck would have it, he told everyone in the class about my picture, and soon they were all calling me the Birdman of Alcatraz—after some old film with Burt Lancaster. So I began to get very isolated. I hadn't met Mitzi then, and was lonely as hell. I would have given anything to have had a friend to go shooting with, both of us with cameras slung round our necks and equipment packs on our backs, but there wasn't anyone. When I was twelve I had tried to make friends with people in the local Audubon group, who have expeditions over on Shelter Island, but these people are all around forty years old and are obsessed with their "life lists." These lists are compilations of all the birds they have seen in their lifetimes, and the club members take the whole thing very seriously. But I wasn't interested in lists. What I was interested in was having a friend.

19

In one sense, my passion for birds has isolated me from everyone. But in another sense, it's the only thing that makes me happy. Father won't even come into my room anymore because he thinks it looks so peculiar. I've papered one whole wall with bird photos from magazines, and my feather collection is now housed in an old curio cabinet that I bought at an auction. I have pheasant feathers, bluejay feathers, iridescent feathers from grackles, and one huge feather that a swan molted last year down by the town pond. This feather collection is a real bone of contention between me and Father, but I refuse to give it up.

I'm a very tidy person, which is fortunate because I own so many nature magazines, so many photo magazines, and so many books on wildlife. The photographers I admire are probably known only to me and a few others—but their names are Thase Daniel, who recently did a book on great egrets that is fantastic, and Eric Hosking. Hosking lost his left eye while photographing an owl (the bird attacked him) but he is still working and shows absolutely no self-pity. The wonderful thing about these people's lives is that they get to go to places like East Africa and the Galápagos Islands. Some even go to the Antarctic every year, to photograph penguins and seals.

At any rate, all the important things that happened to me began last April—the first thing being the return of the three mallard ducks. "Mrs. Woodruff!" our North Haven maid, Ethel, yelled to my mother. "Those awful ducks are back."

Mother went out to the terrace to investigate, a glass of grapefruit juice and vodka in her hand. "Well, I declare," she said, "they're back. Tyler!" she called. "Tyler, honey! Your ducks are back."

It was eleven o'clock on a Saturday morning, and I was just coming out of the shower. I put on a bathrobe and ran outside. "I don't believe it," I said.

Mother and I looked at each other. Because we were both thinking of Father, and what his reaction would be. These three ducks, two males and a female, had appeared on the terrace exactly a year ago—and against Father's wishes I had fed them. First the two males had mated with the female, then they had spent weeks protecting her as she ate and ate, and got fatter and fatter, and prepared to lay eggs. I fed them cracked corn and birdseed, and kept a bowl of water on the terrace for them—and of course I took hundreds of pictures. But Father was edgy about the whole thing. Ducks make a certain amount of mess, though personally they are quite clean, and also, the female duck developed a kind of passion for Father. The closer she got to laying her eggs, the more she would follow him around the lawn, and this made him terribly nervous. She just wouldn't leave him alone. Then one morning she disappeared, only to return a month later with five tiny ducklings.

Mother and I were intrigued with all this—me, because it was such a great opportunity to take pictures, and Mother, because basically she is a kindhearted person who loves animals and who wishes that she could have a dog. (Father is allergic to animal dander, so she can't.) But Father worked himself up into a rage over the ducks, almost as though he were jealous of them, so that when the duck family moved down to the cove he was relieved. Now they were back again, on the same date they had come the previous year, and Mother and I were looking at each other.

"He'll be furious," I said. "What time does he arrive today?"

Mother sank down in a deck chair. "Three. The bell tolls at three."

"What do you think I should do?"

"Well . . ." she said. And then I realized how high she was. It was still morning, but she had had a lot to drink.

"I can't turn them away. They've come back here and everything. To breed."

"Oh, honey, just let them stay. We'll work it out."

I leaned down and kissed her, which is a rare thing for me to do. "Thank you," I said.

I ran into the house, to get the cracked corn and water bowl, and when the ducks saw me coming out with the food they quacked with excitement. How amazing, I thought—first of all that they have stayed together for a whole year, and second of all that they remember me.

The three ducks (whom Mother named Groucho, Harpo and Zeppo last spring) ate like crazy, running back and forth to their water bowl to wash the food down—and then they settled on the lawn as though they had never been away. I went inside and got my camera and began to take pictures. I had taken dozens of closeups of these ducks last year without too much success, so this time I decided that I would work on groupings. The light that day was good, and the ducks were cooperating. Then, three hours early, Father arrived.

Mother and I were having a sandwich together on the terrace, with the ducks sleeping nearby, when we heard the Mercedes pull into the driveway. "Oh, my God, he's early," Mother said. "I must look a wreck."

23

"You look fine," I said, but it wasn't true. Her hair was untidy and her face had that sallow look it always gets when she is drinking. We both sat there like stones as Father parked the car and walked across the lawn.

The first thing he saw were the ducks. And the second thing he saw was Mother with her hair a mess and a glass in her hand. The third thing he saw was me—wrapped in an old bathrobe with a camera around my neck. "What's going on here?" he demanded.

Mother jumped to her feet, pretending to be very cheerful. She kissed him and gave a little laugh. "Why, nothing at all, sugar. How was the traffic?"

Traffic is always a good topic to introduce with Father, because he is obsessed with the Long Island Expressway. "It took me three hours," he said. "Who are those ducks?"

Suddenly Mother went into her girlish routine—but I was touched by it, because I knew she was trying to protect my mallards. "Why, darlin', those are the same three ducks that Tyler had last year. And it is a *miracle* that they have survived the winter to return to us. It is practically something Biblical, George. They have returned with the spring!"

"They dirty the terrace," Father said, putting

24

his briefcase down. "They're filthy."

"But sweetheart, Tyler will clean up after them."

Father stood in the middle of the terrace, his shoulders squared as though he were about to make a speech. "Will you tell me," he asked, "what I have done to deserve this?"

"What, honey? Deserve what?"

"Do you know what kind of week I've had at the office? Do you have any *notion* of the week I've had? The office is in such chaos over the Kalgonite takeover that Andrews had to go into something called biofeedback. To calm his nerves."

"Why, how amazing," said Mother.

"What's biofeedback?" I asked.

"Tyler," said my father, "this is not a hotel. Get dressed."

I nodded and went into the house, where I pulled on a pair of jeans and a shirt. But depression was washing over me like waves, because I could see that this was going to be one of those weekends in which Mother kept on drinking and Father kept on complaining. It seemed to me that she drank more on weekends than other times, because Father made her so nervous. If she had had her hair done one way, he would complain that he liked it another way. If she decided to wear slacks to a cocktail party, he would insist that she wear a dress. She just couldn't do anything right, and in some ways I didn't blame her for drinking.

I went off to my Saturday job, which is working for an elderly person named Mrs. Edgeworth—doing her errands and her vacuuming, etc.—and by the time I returned home, around six, I was in a better mood. But things at home had deteriorated. Mother was completely tight and Father was out on the lawn, his face rigid with anger, knocking golf balls around. Unfortunately, the female duck was following him everywhere he went, an adoring look on her face. "Tyler!" he yelled. "If you don't get this duck away from me, you'll be eating it for supper."

I ran over to Zeppo and shooed her away from Father. To my relief, she and the two males took wing and flew down towards the cove. "I think I'll take a walk," I said to Father, but he didn't respond.

I went into the house and put on my rubber wading boots and my safari jacket. I got my binoculars and camera, and some extra film, a bottle of lens cleaner, and my camera bag, and then I took off. I wanted to go look at that nesting swan. I figured it would calm me.

FOUR

It was twilight now, and the light was fading in a very beautiful way. Because we were having such a cold spring, the fruit trees along the road were just beginning to come out—soft white and dusty pink—and a thin layer of fog was drifting in from the harbor. It had finally occurred to me that I could get closer to the swan's nest by circling the pond and taking a narrow path down to the water, opposite to where she was. I wanted a picture of her very badly, and had put fast film in the camera because of the fading light.

I crossed Route 114. There were no cars on the road and not a person to be seen. Everyone was at dinner, I guess, or watching TV. Which made me think about Mother and Father, and the terrible weekend they were about to have. Then I thought about Cameron and his new friend, Vincent. Of all the depressing things in my life, this one was the worst.

What I haven't explained to you is that Mother and I had finally located Cameron at a friend's house, after he walked out on us that night two years ago. But Cameron never came home again, except once to get his clothes, and it made Mother very unhappy. I think that eventually he would have liked to come back to visit, but Father wouldn't have him in the house. I couldn't understand this until I eavesdropped one night and heard Father telling Mother that he would *not* allow Cameron to have a bad influence on me. (Which is crazy, of course. Completely unrealistic.) So Cameron was banished from the apartment and the North Haven house, and even the place down in Florida, which none of us ever use.

I began to have secret meetings with Cameron whenever I went to the city. We met at places like the Museum of Modern Art and the Plaza Hotel, and he would always treat me to a very good time—lunch, theater matinees, things like that. We saw *Cats* together, and a couple of tremendous photography shows. We went to the Museum of Natural History, and in the summers we would walk around Greenwich Village. But things were different now, because I knew very little about his life or what was going on with him. The only personal thing he told me was that he had borrowed some money from our cousin Lewis, who is a lawyer, so he could survive.

One day we were sitting in the bar of the St. Regis Hotel, Cameron having a glass of white wine and me having a Coke—because it was two days before my fourteenth birthday and we were celebrating—when Cameron said, "Tyler, old buddy, I have something to tell you."

"Oh?" I said, staring at him through the dim light. The bar at the St. Regis has very dim, pink-colored lighting. It made him look odd. And suddenly I didn't want to hear what he had to tell me. Because I knew it was something I wasn't going to like.

"I'm crazy about that bird mobile you made for my birthday," I said, to change the subject. "It's beautiful."

He grinned. "Don't change the subject, Tyler."
"I wasn't."
"Yes, you were. . . . Look, old man, this isn't bad news. It's good news. I've fallen in love."

I was so surprised by this statement that for a moment I forgot he was gay. I know this sounds strange, but I just didn't remember. "No kidding,"

I said. "What's her name?"

A strange look came over his face. "What are you talking about, Tyler? It's a man."

"Oh," I said. "Gee, I'm sorry. My mistake. What's *his* name?"

"Vincent. Vincent Milanese. He's Italian."

I couldn't think of a single thing to say. Because the whole thing seemed too much. I mean, I was lonely enough without having to hear that Cameron was in love with an Italian named Vincent. In some ways, it was the last straw.

"Don't you want to hear about this? It's a very important development."

"Sure," I said. "Sure. Let's order another drink."

Cameron placed the order with the waiter, and turned back to me. "He's an interior designer, Tyler. He's asked me to join his firm."

"Well," I said. "That's nice."

"We're also thinking of living together."

I couldn't think of anything to say. Nothing. So I just sat there.

Cameron reached across the table and took my hand. "I know how weird this must seem to you, old buddy, especially at your age. But Vincent and I are very deeply involved."

Then why don't you go down to City Hall and get married? I wanted to say to him. Why don't you go to Tiffany's and buy rings?

"Do you have to live with him?" I asked.

"I don't *have* to, Tyler. I want to. We're deeply in love."

"Well," I said. "Congratulations."

I knew my reaction was a disappointment to him, but the whole thing was just too much for me to accept. I had a sudden image of this Vincent in some terrible kind of drag. A dress or something.

We finished our drinks and went for a walk up Fifth Avenue—but there wasn't anything to talk about. The news had been a blow to me, and my reaction had been a blow to him. I knew he wanted to talk about Vincent—I knew he wanted to tell me all kinds of things—but I just couldn't listen.

I took the six o'clock bus back to Long Island, and for a change it wasn't crowded. I got a window seat and pressed my face against the glass and didn't move for two hours. I wanted to cry but couldn't, because the tears were too far inside of me, so I just stared out the window at the express-way and waited for the air to change—which it always does when you're getting close to The Hamptons, around Wading River.

Anyway, it was April now and I was plodding down Fresh Pond Road, trying to get close to that nesting swan. I had pretended to adjust to the fact that Cameron was living with a man named

31

Vincent, and Mother (who knew about it too) had also made an effort. Father didn't know, because we never discussed Cameron with him—but the point is, my loneliness was worse than ever. There were times when I thought I would die of loneliness, as if it were a disease. Then I would tell myself that it didn't matter, and that I was better off as a solitary person because of my photography. But there were days when I needed to talk to someone and show them my pictures. Mother wasn't the right person, because she thought everything I did was wonderful. Even in kindergarten, when I would bring home these terrible finger paintings, she would say, "Why, honey, that's the most beautiful thing I've ever seen in my *life*," so that her attitude was rather biased. She was the same way about Cameron. Whatever he did was the greatest.

I walked to the opposite side of the pond— which is a very large one—and took the path that led down to the water. The evening was becoming more and more beautiful, and an owl was hooting somewhere. A group of black-and-white eider ducks was playing in the water, and now I could see the male swan swimming around the little island, very alert, very protective.

I slipped the lens cap off the camera, and saw that the male swan had climbed up on the nest with his mate, and that they were rearranging the nest materials together. What a shot! I said to myself, as I started to focus my zoom. But—believe it or not—I still wasn't close enough, or rather the lens wasn't long enough. I took the picture anyway, but with a sinking heart, because I knew how tiny the swans would look when the film was developed. It was a goddam shame.

That night I lay in bed inventing the names of ice creams—and each name that came into my mind had a check for a thousand dollars attached to it. Maple Walnut Wallop? I said to myself. Chocolate Concerto? What about Bracing Butterscotch or Marshmallow Madness? Not good enough, not good enough. What I needed was something so brilliant it seemed simple. "Less is more," Cameron was always saying. "Simplicity is the key."

FIVE

It was May and I was sitting on the lawn with Groucho, Harpo and Zeppo. They had eaten themselves into a stupor and had fallen asleep with their feet tucked up. I myself hadn't slept well for nights because of thinking about Cameron. By now, he and Vincent were living together, and working together, and though they had asked me to visit them a dozen times, I couldn't bring myself to do it. I kept wondering which one of them did the cooking and housework, and how they made love and everything—and these thoughts were disturbing.

Also, there had been a scandal in The Hamptons during the past week, and the nature of this particular scandal didn't help my peace of mind. It seems that the cops broke into a house near East Hampton where a party was going on, and found all these men inside dressed up like women. Makeup, dresses, high heels, the works. The trouble was that one of these men was a New York dentist, and two others were prominent real estate brokers. All of them married and everything. The story even got on the television news, and as we watched it Mother and I couldn't look at each other. We had never talked about Cameron being gay, but I knew that she thought about it constantly. As for Father, I think he was pretending to himself that Cameron was dead. (Much later, Cameron explained to me that transvestism and gayness were not connected. But how was I to know this? I wasn't planning to be a sex therapist. I was planning to be a photographer.)

Even the coolest people were shocked by that dress-up party. And of course, when the cops busted in they found a lot of coke. Cocaine is everywhere, along with the other usual drugs, and even at my school you can buy whatever you want. Almost everyone deals, or so it seems. But I had never been into drugs, and the way Mother drank had turned me off alcohol. Which left me without any kind of escape. Drugless in The Hamptons, so to speak.

It is possible to think of The Hamptons as a place where people come to fall apart under the pretense of having a good time. I mean, so many of the summer people are drinking and drugging themselves to death, or sleeping with everyone in sight, or driving around stoned in very beautiful cars. The local people, of course, are different, and it was the local people who were my friends. I think it says a lot about me, at this particular time, that my two best friends were the lady who runs the dry-cleaning store in Sag Harbor, and the clerk at the Speedy-Print Photo Shop. Both of them around sixty.

Anyway, it was May and I was sitting on the lawn thinking about my eighth-grade graduation, which was coming up in a few weeks and which depressed the hell out of me. Not that I didn't want to get to high school. I was so anxious to grow up that I would have liked to have taken a pill and become thirty. Instantly. But the point about graduation was that it was connected with all these events. Parties in Water Mill, parties in Wainscott, parties in Montauk. And I was invited to only one of them, and that was probably a mistake on the part of somebody's mother. I might as well have been invisible for all the social life I had, and things had always been this way. It wasn't that I was shy, it was simply that I was different—and a teenager who is different pays a price. For example, just last year a disco opened in Sag Harbor that is exclusively for people twelve to sixteen. They don't serve liquor or anything, but it's a place for kids to go, and dance to live music, and meet each other. Well, I went to this place once, just once, and it was a mistake. Nobody spoke to me, nor I to them. And after standing with my back against a wall for around two hours, drinking a Coke and pretending to look bored, I just couldn't take it any longer and left.

Cameron used to be just the opposite—friendly, social, gregarious. When I think of all the parties he used to attend, I'm amazed. It was only three years ago that he had a steady girlfriend named Stacy, whom Father was crazy about, and now instead of Stacy there was Vincent. These were the thoughts I was having when Mother pulled into the driveway in her station wagon. It was Saturday morning and she had just gone to town for the mail.

"The town is *filled* with people," she said to me. "In May. It's perfectly awful."

"I know," I said. "Did I get any mail?"

"Why, yes you did, honey. Something from your brother."

"No kidding? How interesting."

Mother gave me a forced smile. "I am so glad

that you boys are keeping in touch."

What Cameron had sent me was the May issue of *New York Interiors*, a magazine that cost six dollars a copy. "Tyler," said the note that was attached to the magazine, "see page thirty. Love, Cameron."

I turned to page thirty and found an article on Vincent Milanese. With photos. The title was, "An Approach to Minimalism: Vincent Milanese's SoHo Experiment."

I began to leaf through the article, growing more and more skeptical. Because the whole thing was devoted to a warehouse in the city that Vincent had turned into a residence for someone. The thing that made me skeptical was that the rooms were almost bare. Big, whitewashed empty rooms with a few beat-up pieces of furniture in them. A painting propped against a wall. A vase of flowers sitting on the floor. The article, however, described all this in glowing terms. Such as, "Restraint and judgement make this living room a paradigm of the new minimalism. The etching is by Dulcy Frankenheimer. The bronze chamber pot is Chinese." Or, "His windows are dressed with blinds instead of fabric; there is textural excitement, but no pattern; the palette is subdued and objects are severely edited."

I finished the article. Then I walked over to the

garbage bin, at the end of the driveway, and put the magazine into a trash can. Because suddenly I hated Vincent Milanese, really loathed him. He sounded like the biggest phony in the world.

The old woman I worked for on Saturdays was in the hospital—so I was at loose ends today. Father was staying in the city for the weekend, Mother was playing bridge this afternoon, and there was nothing on the agenda for me except checking nests. I was watching three different birds on nests—that swan being one of them, and the others being Canada geese—because I wanted to photograph the young when they hatched. I was going through four rolls of film a week, and this film, plus the developing and enlargements I ordered, was costing a lot of money. I thought of that 85–300 lens and all the other things I needed—a plastic rain case for the camera through which you could photograph, a new tripod, and something called a Mini-Vac which was a tiny, hand-held vacuum cleaner for slides.

The first bird I checked on was that swan near Fresh Pond Road. Quiet, absolutely still, her head folded back between her wings. Then I rode my bike over to a pond near the bay beach and looked at the Canada geese. Exactly the same. Asleep, with their heads tucked into their wings, the males patrolling nearby. None of my books explain what goes on with a swan or a goose when it is on a nest, if it eats or drinks, or how it survives such a long inert period. It's a mystery.

I didn't know what to do with myself, so I decided to ride into Sag Harbor and have a chat with Burt, my friend at the Speedy-Print Photo Shop. Burt is not exactly a connoisseur of pictures, and I rarely show him mine, but at least he is someone to talk to.

I rode my bike along Route 114, inventing the names of ice creams. Racy Rum Raisin? Comforting Caramel? What about Peppy Peppermint or Boisterous Boysenberry? Was there an ice cream called Elberta Peach? If so, what about Erotic Elberta? No, I decided. Olsen's was a family restaurant. Erotic Elberta wasn't right.

I was just chaining my bike to a tree on Main Street, near the photo store, when a tiny convertible screeched to a halt in the middle of the traffic and someone yelled, "Tyler! Is that you?" I looked around and saw Stacy Parish waving at me from behind the wheel of an MG. All of which was odd, because I had been thinking about her earlier in the day. She was the person Cameron had gone steady with.

"Hey," I called to her. "What are you doing down here?"

She guided her little MG into a parking space

and jumped out. And all over again, I realized how beautiful she was. Stacy Parish was probably the most beautiful woman in the world—which is why, of course, she had become a model. She was wearing a white pants suit, and dark glasses, and high heels, and her long hair was flowing around her shoulders.

She gave me a hug. "Tyler! How terrific to see you."

"Terrific to see *you*," I answered. "How long are you down for?"

"Just the weekend. Mummy's opening up the house."

"How are things?" I asked.

"Terrific. Let's go have a drink."

We headed for The Cooper Hotel, which is on Main Street and which dates back to 1850. It is a very interesting place, completely refurbished, where people like to have drinks or afternoon tea. Stacy was not a tea person, so we headed for a table in the bar.

She ordered Campari, and I ordered a Coke. Then we looked at each other. "It's been a long time," she said. "You look wonderful."

"You too," I replied, amazed at how glad I was to see her. I mean, she was something out of the past that suddenly seemed important. Her parents have a house in Wainscott, and Cameron and I used to swim in their pool.

"How's New York?" I asked her. "Are you working?"

She gave a little laugh. "Work is not what I'd call it, sweetie. A few industrial shows, a shampoo commercial. That's all."

"Modelling must be hard. The competition and everything."

"Tell me about *you*," she said. "How are your parents? How's school?"

She didn't mention Cameron until she was on her second drink, and then she tried to do it in a casual way. "How's that big brother of yours? Still in Europe?"

"Oh, no," I said. "He's been back for two years, studying interior design and everything. He's, uh, been very busy."

Stacy ordered another drink, which surprised me. I hadn't remembered that she drank so much. "I've heard some rather odd things about Cameron lately. But you know what the grapevine is like. People get everything wrong."

"Sure," I said. "I know."

"I mean," she said, taking a sip of her drink, "not only do people get everything wrong, but they do it in a rather vicious way. Don't you agree?"

I wasn't sure what she was aiming at, so I just nodded.

"Take Barby Fairchild. The worst gossip in New York. You remember Barby, don't you?"

"I don't know. Maybe."

"Well, she's been spreading some rather odd rumors about Cameron. And I think it's too bad."

I knew now what she was referring to. And the minute I knew it, I wanted to leave. All my pleasure in seeing her was suddenly ruined.

Stacy lit a cigaret. "Tyler, you and I used to be buddies. So let me be honest with you. Barby Fairchild is spreading it all over New York that Cameron has turned gay."

"I don't know what you're talking about."

"I think you do, Tyler. At least, you look like you do."

"Sorry. I don't know anything about it."

Stacy was staring at me. "It's all right. I can tell from your face that it's true. Which explains everything, simply everything."

I sat there feeling confused. Because half of me had a certain compassion for her, and the other half of me wanted to tell her to go drown herself.

"I wanted to marry Cameron," she said. "Did you know that?"

"No."

"I wanted to marry him and do the whole bit. Babies, dogs, a house in the country. How laughable."

"Look, Stacy . . ."

"Because as far as I was concerned, Cameron was just the nicest, most attractive, most sensitive person I had ever met. But now everything's clear."

"I have to go now," I said. "I have a couple of things to do."

"Yes," she said, as though I weren't there, "clear as glass. I mean, I'm not exactly ugly. Men want to sleep with me all the time. Constantly, in fact. But not Cameron. Oh no, he was too much of a *gentleman* to make love to me. And now I know why."

"I'm afraid I have to go. Take care, Stacy."

She didn't hear me. So I just walked out of the hotel, and got my bike, and rode back home over the North Haven bridge. A thunderstorm was brewing and the sky was very dark—and I was more depressed than I had ever been in my life.

I parked my bike in our driveway, and instead of going into the house I walked down to the cove, which is a few hundred yards away. I was looking for the three mallards, but the only one I could find was Zeppo, who was sitting on the grass by herself staring out at the water. "Hi," I said to her. "Where are the boys?"

She gave me a bored look and stared back at the water, so I sat down next to her, aware of how fat she was getting, how sleek. I would have like to have petted her or stroked her, but of course that wasn't possible. And though I know it sounds silly, I told her that I loved her.

SIX

Cameron and Vincent were coming to North Haven. I could hardly believe this, but they were coming down the weekend of June 8th. There had been another article about Vincent, this time in *Architectural Review*, and Cameron had sent the article to Mother and Father—making it clear that Vincent was his new friend. It was all about a castle in France that Vincent had dismantled and brought over to Westport, Connecticut. Well, Father has some very good friends in Westport, so grudgingly he read the article. Then Cameron phoned to say hello. Then Mother, in a burst of enthusiasm, put Father on the phone—and that's how it happened. Father softened a little when he heard Cameron's voice for the first time in two years, and Cameron was especially friendly. Then *I* got on the phone, and Cameron said, "I think I've broken the ice, Tyler. I think he's coming round."

So they were coming down on June 8th, just for the day, and Mother was excited about it. She and Ethel, our maid, washed and ironed all the curtains, and waxed the floors, and acted like royalty was coming. As for Father, he was quiet and sullen, the way he always is, but I knew that the event meant something to him too. I could see the conflict that was going on inside him. Half of him was looking forward to seeing Cameron, and the other half disapproved of the situation deeply because of his conviction that all gay people are subhuman. You know. The kind you see wandering around 42nd Street and Broadway in the city—weird and stoned and being prostitutes or something. It would have been useless to tell Father that Michelangelo was gay, and Walt Whitman, and J. Edgar Hoover (all of which I learned much later, and which he wouldn't have believed anyway).

To understand Father, you have to realize that he is a perfectionist, and that this perfectionism tends to drive him crazy. It is not unusual for him to walk around the house looking for dust.

47

I mean, he even draws his finger along the furniture, to see if he can make a mark, and if there *is* some dust he is enraged. He also insists that our lawn be mowed twice a week in summer, and I have waxed the Mercedes for him so often that it shines like glass. There always have to be clean sheets on beds, and fresh towels in bathrooms, and this amuses me since the essentials of life—like heat in winter—are often skimped on. I think the problem is that his father was a perfectionist too, and tortured him with high standards.

A lot of things had happened since I had had drinks with Stacy Parish. First of all, I had graduated from the eighth grade, and as I mentioned earlier there had been all these parties. If I had known Mitzi then, I wouldn't have given a damn about it—but as things stood I almost felt like I was graduating alone. Then there was the fact that Mr. Edwards, who owns the Speedy-Print Photo Shop, had put one of my pictures up on the wall of his store. An 11 × 14 enlargement of two deer standing in the woods. This shot was pure accident, like most of my work, because deer are very hard to approach. They either hear you or smell you. But I had come upon these two so suddenly that they had frozen, and by luck I was able to focus quickly and shoot quickly, and the result was very beautiful. Two young white-tailed deer in the middle of the spring woods, with the leaves just barely out.

Because, of course, I do other animals besides birds. Raccoons and foxes (when I can find them) and last year two muskrat twins that I discovered in a pond—diving and swimming and having a great time, with their mother watching nearby. When really hard up, I do cats and dogs, but somehow never find them interesting. I got a shot of a hawk once, carrying a dead mouse in its talons— but as usual, my lens wasn't long enough to get a good picture.

One last thing about my graduation, and then I'll drop the whole subject. The ceremony took place in a building on the grounds of our school called the Manor House, and as I stood there on the platform with everyone else, I realized what the worst part of it was. The worst part was that Cameron wasn't in the audience. Mother and Father were there, and Ethel our maid, and even Burt from the photo store—but Cameron was absent. And as the music began and the school chorus burst into song, I realized that Cameron had always been a buffer for me. Everyone was impressed with him, and sometimes when things got rough all I had to do was bring him along and there would be a change in the air. A kind of electricity. When I was in the fourth grade, at the Spencer School in New York, there had been a boy named Wally Seaforth who used to torture me and steal my possessions, a very good Swiss Army Knife in particular. Well, I told Cameron about it, and the very next day he picked me up at school on 85th Street. "Which boy is it?" he asked, and I pointed to Wally, who was loitering outside, talking to some kids and trying to show off by smoking a joint, which no one did in those days. At least, not in the fourth grade.

Cameron walked up to Wally and looked at him. "May I speak to you for a minute?" he said. "It's rather important."

Wally said sure, and he and Cameron went over and sat on a bench on Fifth Avenue, near the park. Cameron was talking nicely, very calmly, but Wally had gone white as a sheet. In fact, he looked a little ill. Then they both stood up, and Cameron offered his hand, and Wally took it and shook it nervously, and hurried away. The minute Cameron came back across the street, I asked him what had happened. But Cameron just winked at me. "Don't worry about it," he said. "The matter is closed." Months later I learned that he had told Wally—in the most cheerful way, of course—that if he didn't leave me alone, he would have him arrested for harassment, tried in court by our cousin Lewis, and that the sentence could easily be fifty years to life. "Up the river."

Wally Seaforth never bothered me again. In fact, he made a point of staying out of my way—and it was things like that that had made Cameron important to me. I may have been weird and unattractive, and different from other people, but none of it mattered as long as Cameron was around. But now he wasn't, and I was standing on that platform feeling more isolated than I had ever felt in my life. The whole day was a bust, and that's the last I'm going to say about it.

Zeppo still hadn't had her ducklings, but she was growing extremely nervous and tense. I kept hoping that she would build her nest in the woods, which were safe, instead of on our lawn, which wasn't. I had finally done a portrait of her that was excellent, a head-and-shoulders shot of her settled down in some leaves, with the light dappled all around her. If a duck could be said to look intelligent, Zeppo looks intelligent in this picture. Her head is turned to one side, and her eyes are sparkling and inquisitive.

I had spent the last few days waiting for phone calls in response to my ad in the newspaper. In the "Jobs Wanted" column. My ad said that I would do gardening and lawn care, carpentry and pool maintenance, errands and vacuuming. But so far I had only received three calls, and all of them backed down when they found out how old I was. Very few people want hired help as young as me. Also, the competition for summer jobs in The Hamptons is fierce.

I was beginning to panic about money—in the sense that my photography was costing more than I was earning. I always get money for birthdays and Christmas, from relatives, but I was going through it like wildfire. My only hope of becoming solvent was that ice-cream contest. But to tell you the truth, my imagination was waning. In the past week I had come up with Blueberry Blast and Proverbial Peanut Butter—but that was all. A thousand dollars was a lot of money, and it would not only buy my new lens and some other equipment, but pay my debt at the Speedy-Print Photo Shop. (I was in arrears there for fifty dollars.)

Better Butter Brickle? I said to myself, as I mowed our lawn. Charming Chocolate Chip? No, definitely not.

And then it hit me. Crazy Vanilla.

The minute the words came into my mind, I knew they were right. First, because they were so simple. And second, because vanilla is a flavor that very few people would think of for a contest. Vanilla is a humble flavor, but it is also very American and very basic. And by adding "crazy" to it, I had come up with something original. Crazy

Vanilla, I kept saying to myself, as I pushed our power mower up and down the lawn. Crazy Vanilla. It was wonderful and I loved it. And for a moment ten one-hundred-dollar bills hovered in the air, right before my eyes.

SEVEN

It was the evening of June 7th, the night before
Cameron was coming to visit, and we were all
in the living room. Father—who had come down
early for the weekend—was slumped in his favorite chair, reading the *Times*, and Mother was dancing by herself to an old Bing Crosby record. A
78 rpm, if you can believe it. The song she was
dancing to was "Pennies from Heaven," which
had been popular when she was a child.

So there we were, like three people on desert
islands, Father reading, Mother dancing, and me
looking at some slides on a little hand projector
that I own. Mother had had a bit to drink because

she was looking forward to seeing Cameron the next day (she drinks when she is happy, and she drinks when she is sad, it hardly matters). She was doing a slow foxtrot around the living room, singing in a husky voice and trying to have a good time.

"AT&T is up three points," Father said. He was, of course, reading the financial page.

"No kidding?" I said. I didn't really know what he was talking about, and anyway I was studying a slide of Zeppo waddling across the lawn.

" 'So when you hear it thunder, don't run under a tree!' " Mother sang. " 'There'll be pennies from heaven for you and me.' " The record ended, and she went over to the stereo to put it on again.

"Kathy, for God's sake," Father said. "You've played it three times."

Mother laughed nervously. "Sorry, honey. I'll play something else."

She put on another old 78, and started to dance again.

"I wish to God tomorrow were over," Father said. "I'm not looking forward to it."

Mother stopped dancing. "Why, George, that's a terrible thing to say. Tomorrow's going to be just lovely. The four of us together again."

"The *five* of us. You forgot the decorator."

Mother sat down in a chair. "His name is Vincent, honey. And he's not a decorator. He's a designer."

"What happens when our friends get wind of this? People ask me about Cameron constantly. What happens when they learn that he's living with a man?"

"Young men have roommates all the time," Mother said defensively.

"Except that this one isn't a roommate. Where did I go wrong, Katherine? Tell me."

"It isn't a question of . . ."

"Cameron wasn't this way as a child! Something must have happened to him when he went abroad. As a child, he was all boy."

"Oh honey, you're just so prejudiced," Mother said.

Father threw his newspaper down. *"Prejudiced?* With people dying like flies from AIDS? You don't even know what you're talking about, Katherine. As usual, you don't know the issues."

It was starting again—this awful discussion about Cameron—and I just couldn't listen. So I put away my projector and left the room. Nobody saw me go, and as I slipped outside I could hear Father's voice getting louder and louder.

I walked down to the cove and stood on an old dock that is crumbling and which somehow never gets repaired. It was a cool clear night, and the lights of the Sag Harbor motel were twinkling like jewels. I heard a duck quack out on the water, and wondered if it was Zeppo and if she was all right. Then all of a sudden life seemed so difficult that I just felt like giving up. People didn't understand each other because they were stuck in their private worlds, involved in a context that had nothing to do with anyone else. And how could you understand another person's context? You couldn't.

I went back to the house—and though it was only nine o'clock, I went to bed. I was beginning to dread tomorrow like I had never dreaded anything. Because I had a feeling that Father was going to behave badly.

EIGHT

At eleven the next morning, Mother and Father and I sat like statues on the front terrace. The dining table indoors was set with Mother's good majolica plates, and the house was filled with fresh flowers. Ethel had agreed to serve lunch, and no detail had been overlooked. Also, the three of us were more dressed up than usual—me in slacks and a white shirt, Mother in a flowery cotton dress, and Father in some very good tan trousers and a pale blue shirt. Some of Father's clothes are so old that they are practically out of F. Scott Fitzgerald, but these clothes weren't. He almost looked handsome.

Fortunately, the three mallards were down at

the cove, so I didn't have to worry about them messing up the terrace or the lawn. For one moment, I wondered why this whole event was taking place. Then there was the sound of a car in the driveway.

I have to pause here to tell you that in the seventh grade I had a teacher named Mrs. Beck, who always used to tell us to get in touch with our higher selves, our best selves. If we did that, she said, we would go far. Well, as that car pulled into the driveway, and as I realized that I was about to meet Cameron's lover, my higher self disappeared. What appeared instead was my lower self, and this personality wanted the whole day to fail. What I wanted was for Vincent Milanese to be so faggoty that he would offend everyone. Then what I wanted was for Cameron to come home.

I looked around and saw that an Audi 5000 had parked near the garage, and that getting out of it were Cameron and this man. Mother and Father rose to their feet—and, as though everything were happening in slow motion, I saw that Vincent Milanese was not faggoty. Instead, he was a six-foot-tall, dark, handsome Italian man. Older than Cameron. Very well dressed. Smiling.

Mother had put a cheery expression on her face. But Father looked as though the firing squad were coming to take him away. Cameron and Mother hugged, and Father shook hands with Cameron very grimly. Finally, Cameron said, "Mom, Dad, this is Vincent."

Vincent Milanese, up close, was even better-looking than he had been at a distance. He was wearing a beige summer suit, a beige shirt, and an expensive brown tie. His shoes had a high polish on them, and he only wore one piece of jewelry, and that was a heavy gold ring. The funny thing was that he was almost as conservative as Father—all of which I would have found hilarious if the whole thing hadn't been so depressing in the first place.

Vincent bowed and kissed Mother's hand. "Madam Woodruff," he said. "It is a great pleasure."

Mother was absolutely taken aback. First that he was so handsome, and second that he had kissed her hand. She murmured something I couldn't hear.

Vincent turned to Father. "Mr. Woodruff," he said. "A very great honor, sir." They shook hands.

Last of all, Vincent turned to me. We shook hands too, and he said, "Tyler, I am so very pleased to meet you. Your brother has told me about your work."

Ethel hurried out to take orders for drinks, and

we all sat down on the wrought-iron terrace chairs, which are uncomfortable but which Father likes. Cameron and Vincent had chilled white wine, and Mother—who, amazingly enough, had not prepared herself for this occasion with vodka—had white wine too. Father and I had iced tea.

I was sure that things were going to be awkward for a while, but they weren't. Mostly, because Vincent was so pleasant and talkative. He had a very soft Italian accent, which made him easy to listen to, and of course, being a designer, the first thing he mentioned was the house. "How charming this is," he said to Mother. "And so beautifully restored."

"The building is 19th century," Mother replied.

"A carriage house?"

"Oh, yes," said Mother. "Yes, indeed."

"You have brought great taste to it, Madam Woodruff. May I ask who did the restoration?"

"Kenyon and Reed," Father said. "In Southampton."

"They are good friends of mine," said Vincent. "We have worked together."

Father was staring at Vincent in a very odd way. He didn't know what to make of him, and his good manners and conservative clothes were probably more upsetting to Father than had Vincent been some kind of freak. As for me, I was feeling confused. I wanted to hate this man, I really did. But it was difficult.

By the time we got to the lunch table and the first course was served, we had all learned that Vincent was from Rome and that he had studied art and architecture at some very famous academy there. Father asked him about his parents—and learned that Vincent's father is called Ernesto Milanese. To my surprise, Father had heard of him, because Ernesto Milanese is the head of a big publishing house called Rondori.

"They've gone into magazine publishing too, isn't that so?" Father asked Vincent.

"Yes, sir," Vincent replied. "And also, newspapers. It is a very large conglomerate."

There was a moment of silence. In a burst of enthusiasm, Mother said, "What a lovely time we're having! I'm just so thrilled that you boys could come."

The meal went quickly, and soon we were all back on the terrace again, as Ethel served coffee. Father offered Vincent a small cigar. Vincent took it, and lit Father's. "Mr. Woodruff," he said, "would you be so kind as to show me your property? The landscaping is exquisite."

Father nodded and the two of them walked away, across the lawn. I could hardly believe my eyes, but there they were—walking together, with

Father pointing out the various things he had done, over the years, to the grounds. I was flabbergasted.

The minute they were out of sight, Mother went into the house and poured herself a huge glass of vodka. When she came back outside, she put her arms around Cameron. "He's *lovely*," she said. "Just as nice as he can be. And so well-mannered."

Cameron was smiling. "I thought you'd like him."

"I'm crazy about him," Mother said. "Why, he could be a movie star."

Cameron walked over to me and put his hand on my shoulder. "Well, Tyler?"

I knew that he wanted me to make some terrific comment about Vincent, but I couldn't. I just gave him a false sort of smile.

Harpo, Groucho and Zeppo were waddling up from the cove, single file, and so I went and got their food and fed them at a distance from the house. I knew that Father wouldn't want them on the terrace, but I was glad to see them all the same. They seemed like a note of sanity.

By the time Father and Vincent returned, they were talking together in a normal way. Father was telling Vincent about the various flood areas on North Haven, and Vincent was telling Father about new advances in building houses by the water, new ways of doing basements and digging wells. It was the kind of conversation any two men would have together, and I could see that Cameron was pleased. But by now I was wishing that they would leave, because the day was taking some sort of toll on me that I couldn't explain. I felt exhausted and wanted to get my camera and head for the woods. But just as it looked like Cameron and Vincent would go, Vincent said, "Tyler, would you be so good as to show me your pictures? Your brother has spoken of them so often."

The last thing in the world I wanted to do was show Vincent Milanese my photographs. I mean, he is a very professional person, and many of my pictures are not that great. Seeing that I was hesitating, he said, "I would consider it a great favor."

So I had no choice but to take him and Cameron up to my room, which is a big loft on the second floor of our house, with windows looking into the trees. "Tyler never puts his work up on the wall," Cameron said to Vincent. "He's very modest."

I opened my supply cabinet and took out a pile of 8 × 12 enlargements. Photos of deer, photos of swans, photos of egrets and herons. Photos of bitterns building nests and tiny tree swallows mating. Suddenly, the whole thing seemed ridiculous.

Vincent studied the photos. "But these are superb," he said quietly.

He sat down at my desk and spread out the pictures. "You work with a zoom lens?"

"Well, yes," I said. "But a very limited one."

"Filters?"

"Only a skylight filter, which everyone uses, I guess."

"How did you obtain this shot?" Vincent asked. He was referring to a closeup of a great blue heron.

"Pure accident. It was feeding in some shallows at the town pond. It didn't see me."

"Amazing," he said. "Quite amazing. Have you ever thought of working in a larger format?"

The thing that confused me was that he meant it. He was completely sincere, and I didn't know whether to be happy or sad. A few minutes later we were all saying good-bye on the lawn—everybody acting friendly and natural, and not as though the day had been an effort. As Cameron and Vincent's car rolled away, Mother gave an enormous sigh. "What a lovely day that was," she said. "What a very lovely day."

I was watching the car disappear down the driveway, heading out towards Route 114. And as it disappeared, something in me disappeared with it. I didn't know what this thing was, but I knew that Cameron was no longer a part of my life. At least, not like before. Cameron and Vincent would probably come to North Haven again, and maybe someday all of us would be one big happy family. But something important and something deep was gone.

"I think I'll go for a walk," Father said, which made me know he was upset. Whenever something upsets him, he goes for a long walk. I watched him stroll down towards the cove, and across the field next door.

Mother was collecting glasses on the terrace, and emptying ashtrays—and Ethel was finishing up in the kitchen. I didn't know what to do with myself, so I went back up to my room and looked at the photos Vincent had admired. In my mind's eye I could see him and Cameron arriving in the city in their Audi 5000 and going out to dinner at some expensive restaurant. Then I saw them going home together, to their apartment on West 12th Street, like some sort of married couple. It was strange and it was terrible—and most of all, it had wrecked my life.

NINE

It was a few days later and I was talking to Burt, the man who works at the Speedy-Print Photo Shop. Burt is not exactly a genius, and he doesn't understand my photos ("You should do *people*," he always says, "not birds") but he likes me and is my friend. Today we were talking about the huge influx of summer people that was swallowing up Sag Harbor. It was still early June, but the streets were jammed and Mother kept complaining that there was no place to park and that the grocery store was too crowded. In addition to which, a movie crew was shooting a film in town and had rented the entire Cooper Hotel through August. "Didn't used to be this way," Burt said to me. "Town used to be peaceful."

"It's true," I replied.

We were sitting in the back of the store having a cup of coffee together because business was slow. Burt, who is around sixty years old, is an odd person to work in a photo store because he's not interested in photography—but he is disabled and needs money, so Mr. Edwards hired him. When I first showed him my pictures he was very polite, but I could see that he didn't dig any of them. "Well, what do you know?" he would say. "A robin. Big as life."

"This used to be a factory town," Burt was saying. "In the last century. Did you know that?"

"Sure," I said.

"An old factory town, filled with poor people. Factory workers, fishermen, that's what the town was. The *Hamptons* was something else, something for rich folks. Now the whole damn place has gone haywire."

"I agree," I said.

"Take them movie stars who come down here for the summers. Now I grant you that they spend a lot of money, which the locals like. But they're a bad bunch, in my opinion. Drinking, drugs . . . makes you wonder what this country's coming to."

"Everyone takes drugs. It's worldwide."

"Nobody *I* know. The wife and me, we don't even take an aspirin unless it's needed. Tell me two people you know who take drugs."

Well, of course, I couldn't think of anyone—having been put on the spot like that. And as Burt continued his tirade about drinking and drugs, my mind went back to Cameron. What I had realized, the day after our luncheon with him and Vincent, was that I had believed that this relationship was temporary, and that sooner or later Cameron would come home. It had taken seeing Vincent in the flesh to know I was wrong. But mostly it had taken seeing the two of them drive away in their brand-new Audi 5000. I kept telling myself that I would adjust to this, that it was simply a part of life, but I wasn't adjusting at all.

"This town used to be a quiet place to live in," Burt was saying. "No motels, no restaurants along the wharf, nothing. Now they got all these antique stores selling God knows what. Stuff you used to throw out of your attic."

"Burt," I said, getting to my feet, "it's been nice talking to you. But I've got to be going."

He squinted at me over his eyeglasses. "Where to, Tyler?"

"I've got some things to do."

"I bet you're off to take some pictures of birds. Am I right?"

I laughed. "Well, yes. Sort of."

"Damnedest thing I ever heard of. A young boy being hipped on birds."

"I know," I said.

"You need some friends your own age, Tyler. You spend too much time alone."

"Right. Well, so long, Burt."

He patted my shoulder. "Drop in tomorrow. We'll talk some more."

"I'll do that," I said.

I had gone to the store in the first place to buy some film, because those swans near Fresh Pond Road had had their cygnets and I was desperate to photograph them. I hadn't realized that the eggs had hatched, but three days ago, at twilight, I had gone down to my usual place near the pond, and instead of sitting on the nest the two swans were swimming. And with them, I could see five little gray heads bobbing along in the water. It was the first time I had ever seen this, so I was very moved.

My problem was how to photograph the cygnets while they were still tiny. The parents were being very protective of them, keeping them close by their sides, even when they tipped upside down to pull up weeds for them to eat. In the late afternoons they would lead the five babies onto the island, to take a nap, and the mother would spread her wing over them to shield them from the sun. The whole thing was miraculous, if you don't mind my saying so, and my need to get pictures was almost physical. I mean, it gave me a tightness in my stomach.

I wondered if any of the people who lived along the pond were watching this spectacle. Probably not. Because it is amazing how little most people see. For example, one day last fall there was an enormous great blue heron standing by the edge of the road, on Route 27, yet nobody saw it. Cars kept whizzing by as though there were nothing there, and yet it was the largest heron I had ever seen in my life. And also, a confused heron—because it stood on the side of the road for at least an hour. Totally unlike this species, which is usually very shy.

At five o'clock I had to do some vacuuming for Mrs. Edgeworth, who was out of the hospital now, so I had two hours in which to photograph the cygnets. It was a beautiful day, with good light, and I left my bike chained to a tree near Route 114. Then I walked down Fresh Pond Road.

Everything was silent, peaceful, calm. No cars, no people, just birds singing and huge white fluffy clouds drifting over the harbor. I circled the pond, took the path down to the water, and saw the swan family.

At first I laughed, because the five cygnets were riding on their mother's back. Then I ripped the lens cap off the camera, focused, and began to shoot. As usual, my lens wasn't long enough—but I kept shooting anyway, knowing that if I got even one good shot I could have it enlarged. The female swan veered suddenly, the babies fell off, and I kept on shooting. Finally, the whole group swam over to the little island and climbed up on it for a nap. The cygnets were the size of kittens.

I sat down at the edge of the pond—realizing that I hadn't sprayed myself for ticks—and put another roll of film in the camera, cursing my inadequate lens. One of my photography books says that zoom lenses are only used by amateurs, but I don't see how else you can shoot wildlife. This book advises using different lenses of different focal lengths, and becoming expert with them. But this same book also advises photographing birds like swans from a canoe. You are supposed to lie down in the bottom of a canoe, drift close to the birds you want to photograph, then pop up and take your picture. All of which seems asinine to me.

By now I had filled out my entry form for Olsen's Annual Ice-Cream-Naming Contest. People are allowed as many entries as they wish, but I had only filled out one because I was positive that Crazy Vanilla would win. In my imagination I had already purchased the new lens, paid off my debt at the photo store, bought a new camera bag, that little Mini-Vac I told you about earlier, and a number of other things I needed. Mr. Olsen would announce the winner in three days, on June 12th.

I want to backtrack for a moment, to tell you what happened the night after we had had lunch with Cameron and Vincent. Father had gone for a walk—making me know how upset he was—and Mother had proceeded to get tight. Ethel had gone home, the house was suddenly quiet, and for dinner we just had scrambled eggs. One of the problems between Mother and Father is that Father doesn't understand alcohol. First of all, he thinks that any addiction can be cured through will power. Second of all, he tends to discuss things with Mother when she is high—which always works out badly.

They were sitting at the dinner table, having their coffee, and I was in the kitchen doing the dishes—but, of course, I could hear what they were saying. It never occurs to them that I have ears.

"You know," Father was saying, "in the old days, if someone had this problem, he would keep it to himself. Not flaunt it."

"What problem, sugar?" said Mother.

"*Now* they want to bring their friends home, into the very bosom of the family. It's crazy."

"I'm sure you're right," Mother said.

"Cameron knows that I would pay for a psychiatrist. The city is filled with top men who handle this problem. One of them has written a book called *The Will to Change.* His name is Heffleburger."

"Oh, yes," Mother said.

"I've read all the literature, and I've called this fellow Heffleburger on the phone. What else can I do?"

"Why, nothing, sugar."

"I can't force Cameron to go. He's a grown man. I can't force him to do anything."

There was a pause, and then Father continued. "Now I don't say that the fellow he brought here wasn't well-mannered. In some ways, he was very presentable. But when our friends begin to get wind of this . . . Kathy, are you listening?"

Mother hiccuped. "Do I have any choice, baby?"

And that's when the mud hit the fan. As the expression goes.

Father realized how drunk she was, how abstracted—and so he went wild. Started to yell and scream and carry on, all of which made Mother hiccup more. She had been drinking since lunchtime.

I stood in the kitchen, up to my elbows in dishwater, and knew that if things didn't improve between them I would have to leave home. What I mean is, run away. In The Hamptons alone I know of three kids who have done this—just disappeared—and at the moment it didn't seem like a bad idea. For one second I had a crazy image of taking Zeppo and hitting the road. All of which is impossible, of course, since you can't really travel with a duck. But I was coming close to hitting bottom, as far as my parents went. I just couldn't take it anymore.

TEN

This chapter is where Mitzi Gerrard enters the story, and I met her on June 12th at four in the afternoon—the day that Mr. Olsen announced the winner of the contest. To begin with, I missed the ceremony at the ice-cream parlor, which is completely unlike me, completely out of character. I was certain the event was going to be at four, when actually it was at two. So I missed the whole thing.

Zeppo had appeared on the lawn that morning—minus any new ducklings—and I hadn't been able to figure out what was wrong with her. She seemed glad to see me, but was very nervous. Almost paranoid. She kept looking from left to right and running in little circles around the lawn. I calmed her down by speaking softly, and at last she settled next to me on the grass. There was a look in her eyes that I couldn't interpret. As though she had troubles I didn't know about. "It's OK," I said to her. "Everything is going to be all right."

The two of us sat there on the lawn, Zeppo glancing from left to right, and me wondering why I was so fond of her. She was only a duck, and yet there was something so vulnerable about her that it touched me. If Cameron had told me once, he had told me a hundred times not to anthropomorphize. Which means, to give human characteristics to animals. "You can't be sentimental about animals," he would say. "It will wreck your photography. Try to detach." But of course, I hadn't learned to do this.

I sat with Zeppo for an hour. Then I went into the house and showered and put on clean clothes—all in preparation for the ceremony at Olsen's. I had it fixed in my mind that the ceremony was at four, and so at twenty to four I got on my bike and rode across the bridge to Sag Harbor. Olsen's is on the wharf, along with a lot of shops and restaurants, and the announcement of the contest winner is the way Mr. Olsen always opens the season.

As I approached the wharf my heart began to

beat very fast. I knew I was going to win, and it almost felt like I was opening on Broadway. Crazy Vanilla, I said to myself for the thousandth time. Crazy Vanilla. It was a brilliant name.

The first thing that seemed odd to me was that the wharf wasn't crowded with people, the way it usually is when Mr. Olsen announces a winner. And the second thing that seemed odd—ominous, really—was that the ice-cream parlor itself was almost deserted. Two people sat at a table having ice-cream sodas, but that was all. No crowd, no hoopla. I couldn't understand it.

I walked up to the counter, where a short, homely teenage waitress was standing, and said, "When are they going to announce the winner? For the contest?"

She gave me a bored look. "That was at two o'clock."

"What?" I said. "What are you talking about?"

"They announced the winner at two. The whole thing is over."

"You must be kidding! I thought it was at four."

"Two," she said firmly. "Two o'clock."

I stared at this girl, who looked around twelve years old, and who had red hair cut into a crew cut. "Then who won? I've got to know."

"It's on the blackboard."

I rushed over to the blackboard, where ice-cream flavors are always listed, and this is what it said. "The winner of Olsen's Annual Sag Harbor Ice-Cream-Naming Contest is . . . Pineapple Pothole!"

I rushed back to the girl with the crew cut and took her by the arm. "What the hell is going on here?"

She shook me off angrily. "What are you talking about?"

"What do they mean, Pineapple Pothole?"

"That's the flavor that *won*. There was a big crowd here at two o'clock. The winner was some fat lady."

"Pineapple Pothole!" I said. "It doesn't even make sense! What kind of a name is that?"

The girl was looking at me like I was psychotic. "It's going to be a scoop of pineapple with a hole in the top—into which they will put a cherry. Pineapple Pothole."

"The whole goddam thing is rigged! I knew it from the beginning."

The girl with the crew cut drew herself up to her full height. "I think you better get out of here," she said. "You're demented."

"To hell with all of you! The whole thing was rigged."

The waitress came around the counter and confronted me. She really was very short. "Look, buster, do you leave of your own free will—or do I call the cops?"

"OK, OK," I said. "I'm just in a state of shock, that's all."

"Why?"

"Forget it. Just forget the whole thing."

Well, for the next few nights I couldn't sleep—I was so angry. Not only was Pineapple Pothole stupid and uncreative, as a name, it was also boring. Who wants to eat a scoop of ice cream that reminds him of a pothole? The injustice of the whole thing made me furious—the result of which was that I developed insomnia. Finally, on the third morning, I woke up at five and decided to go down to the pond and have a look at the cygnets. I rarely photograph that early, but it's a good time. All of the books on wildlife photography tell you to shoot at dawn and at dusk—the hours when birds and animals are most available.

I put on my rubber wading boots and my camouflage jacket—bought at the Army-Navy store—stuffed all my gear into my camera bag, stuck some extra rolls of film into my pocket, and took off. The sun hadn't risen yet, and there was a soft mist close to the ground. I was glad to be out early because I had had a terrible dream about Zeppo—having finally discovered what the matter with her was. To put it crudely, Zeppo was being

80

gang-raped. Which was why she looked so paranoid all the time. I had heard some loud quacking in the bushes yesterday, only to discover Zeppo being attacked by two male ducks. Her own mates, Groucho and Harpo, were trying to drive the intruders away, but weren't having much luck. So I ran into the house, got a bucket of water, and threw it at the intruders—who rose into the air quacking wildly and flew away. Zeppo's mates looked chagrined by the whole event, while Zeppo herself just looked defeated. It depressed the hell out of me.

I took my special path down to the pond and looked out at the water. The sun was rising over Sag Harbor, and it had turned the mist an apricot color. I focused my binoculars and saw that the swan family was still on the island, asleep. A snowy egret was running around in the shallows, trying to catch fish, but I didn't want to use any film on a snowy egret. I was waiting for the moment when the swans would leave the island and slip into the water.

Suddenly I jumped, because I realized that I wasn't alone. About ten yards away from me was a little kid, standing up to his ankles in water. He was watching the swans too, and there was a beat-up camera around his neck. For some reason, this made me wild. I mean, in the context of my entire life it was the last straw.

"Hey!" I said. "You, over there."

He jumped with surprise, turned to look at me— and I saw that it wasn't a little kid at all. It was the very short waitress from Olsen's Ice-Cream Parlor, wearing sneakers and jeans and a shirt that was too big. "What are you doing here?" she said.

I tried to control the rage I felt. "The question is," I said, "what *you* are doing here."

"Taking pictures."

I laughed, but my laugh sounded more like a snort. "With that?"

I was referring to her camera, which was just an old Kodak held around her neck on a ragged leather strap. It was the worst-looking camera I had ever seen.

"Look," I said, "this place is very private to me."

"You own the pond?"

"Well, no, but . . ."

She glared at me. "You're the game warden?"

"Of course not."

"So come off it. Why can't we both take pictures?"

At that moment the male swan rose to his feet, shook himself out, and spread his wings. The female did the same, revealing the five cygnets who had been sleeping under her. The parents preened for a while, then they headed down to the water, the babies following in single file.

I knew my lens wasn't long enough, but I started shooting anyway. I wondered how the waitress from Olsen's was going to get anything with her terrible camera. Then I looked up and realized that she was no longer standing by the pond. She was *in* the pond, wading out towards the island. As the water reached her waist, she balanced the camera on her head to keep it dry. When she was just a few feet away from the swans, she started shooting.

I was dumbfounded. First, because I had never thought of doing such a thing. And secondly, that the swans didn't attack her. She was talking calmly to them, clicking away, and when she had finished her roll of film she turned around and waded back to the little beach. She was soaked, and her sneakers were black with mud. "I got what I wanted," she said. "The light was great."

For some reason, that statement made me furious. "Don't you know there are water moccasins in there?" I said to her. "To say nothing of snapping turtles."

She pulled a cigaret out of the knapsack she had left on shore, lit it, and sat down on the sand. "I've been coming here for years, buster, and I never saw a snapping turtle. Not once."

"Well, they're in there all the same."

She looked at my camera with its zoom lens. "Did you get anything?"

"Of course," I said. "I come here every day, for God's sake."

"So do I."

I stared at this girl, liking her less with every passing minute. She was in no way attractive, and her red crew cut wasn't even punk. It was just a crew cut, the kind a soldier would wear in boot camp, and she had a million freckles. The shirt she had on must have been her father's.

I wasn't sure how to proceed, so I sat down a few feet away from her. "There are a lot of ticks in the grass," I said. "Be careful.

"You know," I continued, "I just can't get over Pineapple Pothole winning that contest the other day. It's such a stupid name."

"You certainly are a bad loser," she said. "You carried on like a maniac."

"A bad loser! You must be kidding. There was a thousand bucks at stake."

"I know. I entered the contest too."

"No kidding! What was your entry?"

"Cheery Cherry."

I winced. "That's terrible."

"So what was yours, big shot?"

"Crazy Vanilla."

"That's pretty terrible too."

I rose to my feet. "I disagree. And if you're going to continue taking pictures down here, I think you should spray yourself for ticks. How come you're photographing swans anyway?"

She shrugged. "Practice. How come *you're* photographing them?"

"I'm on assignment for a magazine," I said. "Nature photography."

I couldn't tell if she believed me or not. It was possible that she did.

She stubbed out her cigaret and rose to her feet. "You seem depressed," she said. Which surprised me.

Depressed? I wanted to say. Why should I be depressed? My brother is living with a man, my parents hate each other, and my pet duck is being sexually attacked in the woods. Why should I be depressed?

The girl put out her hand. "My name is Mitzi Gerrard."

I didn't have much choice, so I took her hand and shook it. "Tyler Woodruff," I replied.

"Are you really on assignment for a magazine?"

"Yes," I said.

"Well, good luck. See you around."

"Right," I said. "And watch out for ticks."

ELEVEN

For reasons that I cannot explain to you, I couldn't get that girl, Mitzi Gerrard, out of my mind. She kept popping into it at the most peculiar moments, like when I was trying to photograph two bitterns on a nest, or when I was taking a shower. She was a very annoying girl, in the sense that she had had no sensitivity about invading my private place by the pond. But on the other hand, I was curious to know why she had been photographing swans. Many people are amateur photographers without being interested in birds, and the more I thought about it, the stranger the whole thing seemed. Her being by the pond at dawn. Her being able to get close to the swan parents. The cygnets were growing fast—nature's way of keeping them alive—and yet the parents were still fiercely protective. One morning they had tried to attack a dog who, innocently, had paddled out to the island to have a look. He got out of there fast.

With these thoughts in my mind I strolled by Olsen's a few days later, and glanced through the big front windows. And by God, there she was, carrying a tray of ice-cream sundaes across the room. She looked tired, and there were beads of perspiration on her forehead. She didn't see me, which was lucky, but my curiosity about her continued. It wasn't that I *liked* her. It was simply that I couldn't figure her out. So I took a chance the next day and set my alarm clock for 5:00 a.m., with the intention of going back to the pond. It was possible that she would be there.

I slept through the alarm, waking up at six instead of five, so I knew I had to hurry. I struggled into my clothes—rubber boots, chinos, camouflage jacket—threw all my gear into my camera bag, sprayed myself for ticks, and at the last moment put a tan hat on my head which is called a Slouch Hat. (I got it from a mail-order place called Jungle Adventure.) Then I had a quick cup of coffee in the kitchen and hurried out the door. I felt very depressed, as I always do in the morning, but today there was a reason for it. For the last two years, religiously, Cameron has phoned me every Saturday, to see how I am. Well, the previous Saturday he had said he couldn't do that anymore. "Let's just phone each other when we feel like it," he suggested—a remark that went through me like a knife. "Fine," I said. "That sounds OK."

There was definitely something wrong with a person who could never tell the truth, I decided, as I hurried down Fresh Pond Road. Hurt my feelings and I'll give you a friendly smile. Wipe me out with a cruel remark, and I'll just shrug. I have never—I mean, not once—been able to show people when they hurt or disappoint me, and this must be some sort of character defect. What I would like to be is a person who can speak up and say, "Hey wait a minute, buddy. You just insulted me," but I suppose that will never happen.

My instinct had been right, because the girl was there—standing by the pond dripping wet. She had been in the water already, photographing the swans, and now she was letting herself drip-dry, so to speak. She was also smoking a cigaret. "Hi there," I said.

She showed absolutely no surprise at seeing me. "Hi. Where've you been?"

"Around. Busy."

She looked at my clothes—the camouflage jacket, the Slouch Hat, the whole works—and said, "Going on safari?"

"Of course not. Don't be silly."

"I got some good shots this morning," she announced. "The cygnets were riding on their mother's back."

"I've seen that a lot of times," I said.

I felt very ill at ease, so I sat down on the sand, wondering what to say to her. As you may have guessed by now, I am not completely comfortable with girls. As a matter of fact, with the exception of the woman who works at the dry-cleaning store, and Ethel, our maid, I have never had a female friend. "That's a Kodak, isn't it?" I said.

"Yeah. Bought it at the thrift shop."

"Does it work?"

"As good as any other. What's that job you're using?"

"A Canon T-50. The lens is a Kiron."

"It isn't the equipment that matters, Woodruff. It's the photographer."

"I don't agree with you," I said. "Even with *this* lens, I have a lot of trouble. Which is why I entered that contest. I wanted to buy a zoom that goes up to 300 millimeters."

"You don't need a 300 millimeter lens. All you

need is a teleconverter."

"What's that?"

She gave me a very calm, very patient look. "It's a little lens you screw onto your regular lens and it doubles the focal length. Just get yourself a 2X teleconverter."

Considering the crummy camera she owned, I was surprised that she knew so much. "You know," I said, "I've been thinking of writing Mr. Olsen a letter about that goddam contest. The whole thing was unfair."

"So when has life ever been fair?"

"I needed to win."

She stamped out her cigaret. "To begin with, Woodruff, you don't look to me like you need money. You look very well-heeled. And also, you've got to learn to be a good loser. Otherwise, you just become a pain in the ass."

"For your information," I said, "I do need money. I'm holding down so many jobs that I practically pass out at night. From exhaustion."

"What do you do? Mow lawns?"

"Among other things."

She sighed. "Look, kid, I've got to get to work. It's almost eight o'clock."

"At the ice-cream parlor?"

"No, at my mother's store. I work there in the mornings, and at Olsen's in the afternoons. On

Saturdays I work at the car wash."

"How did you get so many summer jobs?" I asked.

"I hustled," she replied. "Well, so long now."

For some reason, I didn't want her to leave. Which was funny, because I didn't really like her. "Which is your mother's store?"

"It's the health food store in Sag Harbor. Near the post office."

"I don't know it."

"It's called Mustard Seed. There's a sign out front."

"Oh, right. What do they sell there?"

"A lot of crazy stuff. Come in and see for yourself."

"OK," I said, "I will." And then she was gone, heading up the path towards Route 114, with her clothes still dripping wet.

I watched her go, realizing that I hadn't asked her the one question I had wanted to—which was why she was photographing swans—and also wondering how old she was and where she went to school. She looked twelve, but would have to be older to hold down all those jobs. She was the epitome of a word Cameron used to use all the time—"officious." In other words, she was bossy as hell. I wondered if she photographed in color, or black and white.

By the time I got home, Mother was sitting at the kitchen table having her coffee. It was a weekday, so Father was in the city, and Ethel had not yet arrived to start cleaning. Mother was drinking a big mug of coffee with milk in it, and looking at a photo album.

"Where have you been, darlin'?" she asked, without looking up.

"Out for a walk. Out photographing."

"I just found this old album in my closet," she said. "It's the most amazing thing."

I sat down next to her and took off my Slouch Hat. "In what sense?"

"Well, honey, in the sense that it has pictures of Uncle Willie and Aunt Beatrice in it. *And* Grandy Hopkins. How handsome they all were in those days!"

I don't think I've mentioned to you that Mother is obsessed with her family, the ones that came from Alabama. Most of them are dead now, but she has this big thing about the past.

"I really regret that you never knew these people, Tyler. They were just all so lovely and attractive. Grandy Hopkins, who you don't remember, honey, had her portrait painted by Winkler, the famous artist. She was such a beauty."

Grandy Hopkins was Mother's mother. She died when I was three.

"Well, for heaven's sake," Mother said, turning a page. "Here's a photo of me when I was seventeen. For heaven's sake."

I looked over her shoulder at the picture. It showed Mother leaning against a velvet couch, dressed in a long white frilly dress. She looked pretty.

"That was the year of my coming-out party, the year that Stanton Turner courted me. Your old mom had dozens of beaux in those days, Tyler. Would you believe it?"

"Sure," I said.

"There was Stanton, and Tommy Woolridge, and a perfectly divine young man named Henry Pierson, who wanted to be a writer. And then there was Darrow Jones, who looked like a Greek god and who Mama never liked because she said he was too handsome for his own good. Such beautiful, romantic young men. . . . And then I came East and met your father."

Her voice changed when she said that, so I glanced at her. "Yes," she said, "I came East to go to college and met George Woodruff. He was older than the boys I was used to, and much more serious. And Mama thought his prospects were good, so . . ."

Her voice trailed away and she sat there lost in her own thoughts. And if I had been depressed

93

when the day started, I was now ready to commit suicide. Because what she was saying—whether she knew it or not—was that she regretted marrying Father. She probably regretted having Cameron and me too, if you come right down to it.

TWELVE

The next morning at 9:00 a.m. I parked my bike in front of Mustard Seed, the health food store near the post office. I felt nervous about going inside—then I reminded myself that Mitzi Gerrard had invited me. It wasn't as though I were barging in on her. She had said to come in and have a look around.

The store looked tiny, and when I stepped inside it looked even tinier. There were shelves of bottles and jars, and open barrels of seeds and nuts. There was a refrigerated cabinet with cartons of yogurt inside, and a small marble counter on which two kittens were sleeping. In the back of the store was a kitchen, and towards the front were three tables with checked tablecloths on them. There was no one around, but then I looked into the kitchen and saw Mitzi cooking something over the stove. I didn't want to bother her, so I walked over to a bulletin board and began to read what was there.

The board was covered with people's business cards. But the things they were advertising were bizarre. "Postural Integration and Colon Therapy" said one card. "Certified Rolfing Practicioner" said another. There were cards for horticulturists and astrologers, cards for people who did reflexology and shiatsu—whatever that was. Then my eye caught a sign that said this: "Channeling the Goddess Within. A Workshop by Malika Grossman, Wiccan Priestess and Shamanic Psychotherapist."

> This experiential workshop will teach you how to connect with goddess archetypes for self-healing and personal growth. Participants will explore the symbolism of the Amazon Maiden, Creative Mother, and Wise Woman, and will experience connections with the triple goddess through fasting and meditation.

What kind of place is this? I said to myself, as Mitzi came out of the kitchen. "Hi," she said. "I saw you come in."

She was wearing blue jeans and an old shirt, and had an apron tied around her waist. "So," she said, "what do you think?"

I looked around the store. "Well, I don't know. It's interesting."

"Sit down and I'll bring you some tea. Make yourself at home."

She went into the kitchen and brought out two mugs of tea and some homemade coffee cake. "How long has your mother had this place?" I asked.

"A few years," she said, sitting down at the table with me. "She used to run Natural Encounters, in the East Village. In New York. But it closed."

"How come?"

"It went broke. We're doing better with this one because it's on a smaller scale. Our apartment's next door."

"Oh. Right." I looked at the two kittens sleeping on the counter. "Are those your kittens?"

"Tofu and Wild Rice? Yeah, they're ours. We found them at the dump."

At that moment, Mitzi's mother came into the store.

I have to admit that this woman surprised me. I mean, I don't know what I was expecting, but Mitzi Gerrard's mother was weird. She was small and thin, with red hair cut into an Afro, and she was wearing a cotton skirt that came down to the ground. She was also barefoot. All I could think of was that she must be some kind of left-over hippie. From the sixties. I rose to my feet and Mitzi introduced us.

"Mom, this is my friend Tyler. Tyler, this is my mom."

"Pleased to meet you, Mrs. Gerrard," I said.

She winked at me. "Call me Shirley, sweetheart. We don't stand on formality around here."

She drifted off towards the back of the shop, the pile of bracelets she was wearing jangling loudly. She really was very weird-looking to be somebody's mother.

Mitzi and I sat back down at the table. "What does your dad do?" I asked.

She shrugged. "I haven't the foggiest. He disappeared when I was two."

"No kidding. Gee. Forgive me for asking."

"That's OK, Woodruff, it's no big deal. He used to work for the telephone company." She laughed. " 'A telephone man who fell in love with long distances.' Do you know where that quote is from?"

"No."

"It's from *The Glass Menagerie*, by Tennessee Williams. God, I love that play."

"I've never read it."

"You should. Get it from the library."

"OK. Listen, Mitzi, I keep wanting to ask you something, and then I forget."

"What's that?" she said, eyeing the front door, where a customer had just appeared.

"I keep wanting to ask you why you've been photographing swans."

Her eye was still on the customer, who was browsing around the shelves of vitamin bottles. "Because I'm going to be a wildlife photographer," she said. "Look, I've got to hustle now."

I jumped to my feet. "Right, right. Will you be down at the pond tomorrow?"

"If it doesn't rain." She was heading towards the man who was looking at vitamins. "Can I help you?" she asked.

I left Mustard Seed and went out to the sidewalk. Through the front windows I could see Mitzi waiting on her customer—a fat man who was completely bald. I was amazed by what she had just said, about wanting to be a wildlife photographer. It was a fantastic surprise.

THIRTEEN

Life being what it is, it rained for the next three days. Which means that Mitzi Gerrard did not come down to the pond. I felt self-conscious about going to her mother's store again, so I just kept waiting for the weather to change. I worked for Mrs. Edgeworth, and for another woman in North Haven who wanted her basement cleaned out, but my mind was elsewhere. Because it seemed absolutely amazing to me that Mitzi Gerrard wanted to become a wildlife photographer. The odds of my meeting anyone in The Hamptons who did that kind of work were probably a million to one. Yet here was Mitzi, right in my own backyard, so to speak.

Mitzi was what Cameron would call an anomaly—something that departs from the norm. To begin with, she looked more like a boy than a girl, and secondly she had a very unusual attitude towards life. Then there was her odd-looking mother, and then there was their odd-looking store. Well, it kept on raining—so that Mitzi didn't appear at the pond—but on Saturday it stopped. Mitzi had said that she worked at the car wash on Saturdays, so I decided to ride my bike over to Clarence Street and have a look. And there she was—wearing a gray jumpsuit and soaping cars as they moved towards the car wash building. "All right, folks, step it up, keep moving," she yelled. "You there, in the blue Cadillac! Neutral, no brakes!"

She acted as though she owned the place. And though there were other people working there too, she was the one that seemed to be in charge. I couldn't stop watching her, and yet I didn't want her to see me—so I stood across the street, near the gas station. As the cars rolled up to where she was standing, she soaped them with a long-handled brush and scrubbed their tires. She really had a lot of energy, when you came right down to it.

That evening Mother and Father went out to a dinner party, and as usual they had an argument before they left. Mother had put on slacks, whereas Father wanted her to wear a dress. But when she did put on a dress, he said it was too low-cut. Also, she had had a few drinks to prepare herself for the party—and when he found the glass of vodka sitting on the bathroom sink, he got very angry. I know this sounds peculiar, but every time they have an argument I feel that it's my fault. Totally irrational, of course, but that's how I feel. The minute they left the house, I went into the library to phone Cameron.

The phone rang for so many minutes that I thought he wasn't home. At last he picked it up. Breathlessly. "Cameron Woodruff speaking."

"It's me," I said. "I almost hung up. Where were you?"

He laughed. "In the living room. We're having a few people over for cocktails."

"I just thought I'd say hello."

"Well, I'm glad you did, old buddy. But this isn't the best time."

"Oh. Well. I'm sorry."

"Nothing to be sorry about. What's on your mind?"

"Nothing, really," I said. Which was ridiculous, because I had a lot on my mind. What I wanted to say was, Cameron I've met this very interesting girl. I don't like her personally, but she does wildlife photography, and you know how rare that is. I'm not sure how to make friends with her—because she's so bossy—but she is the first person in my whole life that I've ever wanted to know. So my question is, how do I proceed?

I didn't say any of that. What I said was, "I just called to say hi. That's all."

"Well, I'm glad you did, old man. But why don't we talk tomorrow? I've got to take the hot canapés out of the oven."

"Right," I said. "Of course. Call you tomorrow morning."

For some reason, Cameron's statement that he had to take the hot canapés out of the oven made me feel crazy. I mean, it was such an effeminate thing to say. As though he had turned into a housewife. And for the next two hours, even though I was watching television, all I could hear in my mind was his voice saying that he had to take the hot canapés out of the oven. So I went into Mother's bathroom and took one of her Valiums. I had never done such a thing before, but I wanted some kind of oblivion.

I got it. In the sense that I passed out on my bed fully dressed. Not being a person who takes drugs or alcohol, that Valium hit me hard. I woke up once in the night to hear Father saying something to Mother downstairs, and then I passed out again. When I woke up in the morning, it was 4:00 a.m.

I took a cold shower—to put myself back together—and tiptoed down to the kitchen to make some coffee. In the corridors of my mind, very faintly, I could still hear Cameron saying that he had to take the hot canapés out of the oven—and there was something in me that wanted to banish his voice forever. I mean, I had *had it* where Cameron was concerned. Because even if he had been entertaining two hundred people, he still should have talked to me.

At five-thirty it began to get light outside, and when I glanced out the kitchen door I saw that Zeppo and her mates were there, waiting for breakfast. I gave them some birdseed and fresh water, and two stale croissants, and then I packed up my camera gear, sprayed myself for ticks and took off. I had no idea whether Mitzi would be down by the pond or not.

She was there. At ten of six in the morning. Sitting cross-legged on the little beach, putting film into her camera. There was a cigaret dangling from her mouth, and she looked as though she hadn't been awake for long. She didn't say anything as I sat down beside her, just nodded, so I didn't say anything either. The sun was coming up and a blanket of mist was rising from the water.

"The light is good," she said after a few minutes.

"I agree," I said.

"I always shoot right into the sun, no matter what the books say."

"Me too."

Through the haze I could see the swan parents coming towards us. They sailed through the pink-colored mist like something out of a fairy tale—but there was only one cygnet with them. I gripped Mitzi by the arm. "Where are the others?"

She put out her cigaret and looked through her binoculars. "They're gone. There's only one left."

I focused my own binoculars. "What are you talking about? Where are the others?"

"Killed, I guess. The mortality rate is very high."

"God! What could have killed them?"

"Sea gulls. Foxes. Dogs."

"Maybe they're back in the fog somewhere."

"I don't think so, Woodruff. I think they're gone."

I didn't say anything, but a lump came into my throat as big as a golf ball. By now you have probably realized that I am not a person who shows his feelings easily—but the fact that there was only one cygnet left almost did me in.

Mitzi sighed. "Look kid, it's nature, and there's nothing we can do about it. That's why they hatch so many eggs. So one or two can survive."

I was so upset that I couldn't speak, and my head was turned away.

"It's just nature," she said.

The swan parents glided up to us, with their one remaining cygnet, and Mitzi threw some crusts of bread into the water. "I've been feeding them since last winter. That's why they let me come close."

They ate the bread greedily, and the cygnet ate too. He had almost doubled his size in the past few days and you could see the beginnings of his long neck. Mitzi was taking pictures—clicking away as the swans moved in and out of the sunlight. "Woodruff," she said, "you are the most depressed human being I have ever met."

I was so surprised by this statement that I didn't know how to reply. Instead, I said to her, "How old are you?"

"Fifteen."

"Where do you go to school? Peterson High?"

"Right. And *you* probably go to Country-Day."

"Well, yes."

"It figures."

The swans pivoted and sailed away, the cygnet between them. They kept him in the middle at all times, and I couldn't help wondering how they must feel, having all the others wiped out.

Mitzi was putting another roll of film into her camera. "Do you want to tell me what's bugging you?"

"Not now." And then, to change the subject, I said, "Have you ever been over to Shelter Island? To the wildlife refuge?"

"Sure, lots of times. Shelter Island is filled with faith healers. Did you know that?"

"No."

"It's like some sort of fantasy world over there. Astrologers, healers, everything. I know this because my mother's boyfriend is into faith healing very deeply. His name is Morton."

"Are you an only child?"

"Yes."

All of a sudden I wanted to ask her a million questions. About her childhood, and her father who had disappeared, and her mother's boyfriend. But at that moment she got to her feet and stretched. She was wearing a pair of boy's chinos and sneakers that had holes in them, and an old pink shirt. Her freckles were very pronounced.

"Why do you wear a crew cut?" I asked.

She glared at me. "Why do *you* go around looking like Ernest Hemingway?"

"Don't get mad."

"I'm not mad, Woodruff, but if I want to wear

a crew cut that's my own business. Correct?"

"Sure, of course. Would you like to come to lunch today? At my house?"

She looked at me suspiciously. "Where do you live?"

"Just across Route 114. Near the cove."

"A fancy neighborhood."

"Not really. Why don't you come to lunch around noon."

A huge bird swooped over our heads and landed on a rock in the middle of the pond. "God!" I said. "Look at that hawk."

"It's not a hawk, Woodruff, it's a heron. A yellow-crowned night heron."

"I don't agree with you. I think it's a hawk."

"A *heron*," she repeated. "Look it up in your bird book, if you have one."

"I have dozens of bird books. Why don't you come to lunch around noon?"

"Do I have to dress up?"

"Of course not. Just come as you are. We're very informal."

"I'm allergic to shellfish," she said. "So don't serve me any."

"All right. Would a sandwich be OK? Ice cream? A Coke?"

She nodded. "Which is your house?"

"It's directly across the main road, next to the red barn. There's a sign with 'Woodruff' on it at the entrance to the driveway."

"All right," she said. "See you at noon. But don't serve me any shellfish."

FOURTEEN

At exactly twelve o'clock, Mitzi rode into our driveway on a battered red bike. She had put on clean blue jeans and a shirt, and was wearing an old straw hat. She had also put on lipstick, very crookedly. "What is this place?" she said to me. "Some sort of estate?"

"Of course not. It's just an old carriage house."

"Where's the English butler?"

I assumed she was kidding, but didn't have time to ask because Mother was hurrying towards us. She had been so pleased when I told her that I was having a friend to lunch that she had set up a special table for Mitzi and me on the terrace. With china and linen napkins.

She and Mitzi shook hands, and then Mother led us onto the terrace. "Now you all just sit down and be comfortable," she said. "I'll be back in a jiffy." She hurried into the house, and from the living room I could hear Father saying, "Who is *that*?" and Mother replying, "Shh. It's Tyler's new friend."

Mitzi gazed out over the lawn. "Who mows all this?"

"Me. I clip the hedge, too."

"Very posh, Woodruff. What business is your father in?"

"Stocks and bonds. He's a broker."

"It figures. On the other hand, it has been my observation that rich people are just as screwed up as poor ones. So where's the advantage?"

Mother appeared with a tray of sandwiches, two Cokes, and a plate of cookies. "Now what we have here," she said brightly, "are egg salad and tunafish, both of them on lovely whole wheat. And I will bring you children some ice cream later on."

Through the glass doors that go into the living room, I could see Father watching all this like some kind of spy. He didn't know what to make of it.

"Don't go to any trouble, ma'am," said Mitzi, rising to her feet.

"Trouble! Why, it is a privilege to serve you children on this lovely summer's day."

"She's nice," said Mitzi, when Mother had gone back into the house. "And, boy-oh-boy, does she dote on you."

"Doesn't your mom do the same?"

"Not really. She's too involved with her boyfriends."

"Oh. I see."

Mitzi bit into a sandwich. "My mother goes through men the way you and I go through Kleenex—but it's kind of sad, because every time she meets someone new she thinks this is *it*. Last year it was a flutist named Clarence, and now it's Morton the faith healer. The one I liked best was Garret Smith. He was a novelist."

"Published?" I asked. I was already on my second sandwich.

"Sure. Except that Garret publishes with very small presses. Like the One Potato Press in Idaho. I really loved Garret, but Mom loaned him two thousand dollars that she never got back. That's why we're both hustling these days."

"You mean that's why you're working so hard? To help your mother?"

"Exactly," she said. "Could I have another sandwich?"

After Mother had served us some coffee ice

cream with chocolate sauce on it, Mitzi asked if she could see my photos. My heart sank, because I knew she wouldn't like them, but I didn't want to be rude. So I took her up the staircase to my room.

"Wow, are you neat!" she said, looking around. "I've never seen such a neat room."

"I prefer to think of it as being organized. Not neat."

"So where are the photos?"

She sat down on my bed, kicked her shoes off, and lit a cigaret. I didn't have an ashtray, so I gave her a jar I usually keep pencils in.

"Did you get that lens extender I told you about?"

"Not yet," I said, fumbling around in my supply cabinet. "God. I don't know which of these to show you."

"Why not show me all of them?"

I have to pause here to explain that there was something about having Mitzi Gerrard in my room that rattled me. I mean, you can't spend your entire life as a solitary person and then—suddenly—have a girl sitting on your bed, lighting up a cigaret. It's the way Mother feels when she goes to the city these days. She gets confused because she has grown so accustomed to the peace and silence of North Haven. The last time she went to New

York, to have a permanent at Elizabeth Arden's, she just boarded the two o'clock bus and came right back. "I was disoriented," she said.

Well, having Mitzi Gerrard in my room disoriented me. But I got out a pile of 8 × 12 enlargements and spread them out on my desk.

She walked across the room, the cigaret dangling from her mouth, and looked at the pictures. Then she put the cigaret out in the glass jar. "Show me some more."

I took out six or seven more—swans, egrets, herons, and many photos of Zeppo—and spread them out for her. "They're not very good," I said. "I know that."

She looked at the pictures for such a long time that I realized that no one had ever looked at them that way before. So slowly and carefully. Then she took one, of a swan sitting on a frozen pond in winter, and took it over to the window.

"Woodruff," she said at last, "I think you have real talent. And that's not something I say very often. But you've got to shove all this sentimentality. It's ruining your pictures."

For some reason, my heart was beating very fast. I sat down on the edge of the bed. "I don't know what you mean."

Mitzi sat down next to me. "Don't faint, kid, we're only talking about pictures—not the atom bomb. What I mean is that you want all these animals and birds to be *pretty*. And pretty they are not. Awesome, terrible, cruel, and magnificent, maybe. But not pretty."

"Go on."

"It's like this. The moments you are choosing to photograph are the adorable moments. So that all these pictures are like a Hallmark calendar. But I don't get a real sense of the birds, if you know what I mean."

"You're right!" I said. "Absolutely right."

"If I'm hurting your feelings, tell me."

"You're not. Honestly."

"These swans, for example. They all look like Robert Redford. I mean, they're all posing in beautiful positions. But swans also mate and fight over territory—and when they molt, they're the ugliest things alive. Have you ever seen the swan fights in January and February? Down at the town pond?"

"Yes, yes. Sure."

"Every February I photograph those fights. They're fantastic."

"When did you decide to become a wildlife photographer?" I asked.

"When I was twelve. Someone gave me a book on Africa."

"Do people think you're crazy for doing it?"

She chuckled. "Sure, all the time. But I just tell them to bugger off."

"I'd like to see your pictures," I said.

And then a silence descended over us. It wasn't that we didn't know what to say to each other— it was more like each of us wanted to think, to reevaluate what was going on. Downstairs, I could hear Mother doing the lunch dishes and Father watching baseball on TV. Far away, there was a sound of thunder.

Mitzi rose to her feet. "I've got to be going now."

I turned to her. "My brother is gay," I said. "And it's tearing me apart."

She put her hand on my shoulder. "So let's talk about it. Come over to my house tomorrow night and we'll talk."

FIFTEEN

I was so shook up that evening that I couldn't even watch television. I just kept wandering around the house, up the stairs and into my room, down the stairs and into the library. Mother and Father, for once, were having a peaceful evening—but I couldn't settle down. I kept thinking about Mitzi, and wondering if the difference in our ages was going to ruin everything. If you had asked me what I meant by "everything," I couldn't have told you—but it seemed like a fantastic piece of luck that I had met her, and I didn't want anything to go wrong.

Around eight o'clock I went out to the terrace and began pacing back and forth—thinking about

Mitzi, and also wondering if Zeppo was all right. I hadn't seen her for days. Thunder was rolling back and forth over the bay, and there was an ominous feeling in the air. The door to the living room opened and Father stepped outside. "Tyler," he said, "there you are. I was looking for you."

Instantly, I wondered what I had done wrong. I mean, Father never looks for me unless I have committed some sort of minor crime—like leaving the garage doors open so that raccoons can get in at night and walk all over his car. "Do you have a minute?" he asked. "Are you busy?"

"No, of course not," I replied.

We began to stroll down towards the cove. Near an old stone bench, Father paused to light his pipe. "Tyler," he said, "I need your advice about something."

Well, you could have knocked me over with a feather. Father needing advice? The King of Wall Street? One of the things about Father that makes him so difficult is that he thinks he is right one hundred percent of the time. But here he was, about to ask my advice, and it startled me. For one moment my whole life passed before my eyes—and what I saw was a completely inadequate son who had a brilliant father whom he was always letting down. I had let him down when Mrs. Blampin, my seventh-grade science teacher, had caught me cheating on a test—the only time I had ever done such a thing—and I had also let him down when I had stolen from the Sag Harbor dime store. Once again, it was the *only time* I had done such a thing, and I was six years old to boot, but when Father discovered what I had taken he acted like I had broken into Tiffany's. He made me go back to the dime store and return the thing (a little plaster mouse) and say that I was sorry. And then he hadn't spoken to me for weeks. So there I was, at the age of six, feeling like I had a criminal record and that I would be on parole for the rest of my life.

"I'd be glad to give you some advice," I said, as we both sat down on the bench.

"Good, good," he replied. "Because there's something on my mind, Tyler, and I think you can be helpful about it."

I was certain that he wanted to talk to me about Cameron, or maybe Mother's drinking—so I sat very still, waiting for what he was about to say. He was looking sort of English, in slacks and an old sweater, and the pipe he was smoking added to the effect.

"Do you think we should build a swimming pool?" Father said at last. "Near the cove?"

"What?" I said.

"Your mother wants me to build a swimming

pool down near the water—but as usual, your mother doesn't know what things cost. The whole idea seems ridiculous to me. I mean, after all, Tyler, how many of us really *swim*?"

"Well . . ."

"Your mother is a poor swimmer, and I'm only here on weekends, and as far as I can see, *you* always swim at the beach. Cameron, of course, is living in the city now, so who would benefit from a swimming pool?"

"Actually . . ."

"Pools require a lot of care," Father continued. "To take care of a pool, you need a pool service. But the main thing is the cost. It would take at least fifteen thousand to build a decent swimming pool, and I can think of many better ways to invest fifteen thousand dollars. Your mother thinks that it will add to the value of the property, add to the base, but since I don't intend to sell the house, what does it matter?"

I just kept nodding while he talked, like some kind of automaton. Because a part of me had simply turned to stone during this discussion. I looked at Father, who was involved in his own thoughts, and then I looked at the house and had an image of Mother inside, drinking her vodka and watching Channel 13 on TV. Then—for the very first time—a voice inside of me said, "Tyler Woodruff, whatever you want from life, you're not going to get it here. It's time to give up as far as these people are concerned, because none of you will ever connect. You're blood relations, all of you, two parents and two kids, but none of you will ever ever connect."

SIXTEEN

The following night I sat on Mitzi Gerrard's bed looking at her photographs. They were the most interesting pictures I had ever seen, but I'll get to that part in a minute. I had been nervous about dropping in on Mitzi, but she was expecting me. The thing that was a surprise was the terrible apartment she lived in. I had rung the doorbell at the building next door to Mustard Seed, and had proceeded up the stairs to a tiny, dingy, cluttered apartment. There was actually more clutter than apartment, if you know what I mean, and Mitzi's mother and her boyfriend didn't even get up when I came in. They were sitting on the couch together, listening to tapes of some very weird music, while the kittens, Tofu and Wild Rice, raced around the room. Mitzi's mother was wearing a blue bathrobe and her feet were bare. Morton the faith healer had long hair and a blond beard, and looked a little like Jesus. "Hey, man," he said as I walked into the room. "Hey," I said. But I didn't sound convincing.

There were only three rooms in the apartment, the living room and two bedrooms, and no kitchen. Mitzi's room was so small that the only place to sit was the bed, and most of her possessions were piled up on the floor. She had some interesting posters on the wall, however, of East Africa, and I was impressed by the fact that she had turned her bathroom into a darkroom. Since she only worked in black and white, it was possible for her to do her own developing.

I was looking at her pictures. Pictures of hawks carrying dead mice in their talons as they flew over the beach. Pictures of swans fighting, swans mating, and one fantastic picture of a swan skidding to a stop on a frozen pond in winter. Its wings were beating hard as it came in for a landing, and the sun was shining through them. There were pictures of the two kittens, and a picture of some stray dogs at the dump fighting over garbage. But the picture that affected me the most was simply a picture of a dead sparrow, lying in a New York

City gutter. People were passing, and cars were rolling by, and yet no one noticed it at all. "Did you take this with your Kodak?" I asked.

"No," she said, "a Nikon with a zoom lens. I used to have some very good equipment, but I sold it last year—when Mom got herself into debt. It doesn't matter. As soon as we're solvent, I'll get myself a decent camera again."

"Your mom seems to have a lot of trouble." I didn't want to say anything tactless, but it upset me that Mitzi had had to sell her Nikon.

Mitzi sighed. "The word trouble doesn't cover it, Woodruff. Every two or three years she opens a new health food store, but then either it goes bankrupt, or the rent is raised, or we lose the lease. And then we have to start over. A new town, a new place, a new boyfriend. The thing that's so weird is that she just can't see what she is doing. I mean, we always wind up back at square one. Broke."

I stared at the picture of the dead sparrow. If my own pictures were too pretty, it was possible that Mitzi's were too bleak. Yet I had to admit that they were strong. "I think your pictures are beautiful," I said.

She went over and closed the door. Then she lit a cigaret. "Thanks, kid. I'm closing the door because my mother goes wild when I smoke. But what can I do? I smoke and drink coffee and love sweets. All the things she's against."

She found an ashtray and sat down on the floor, looking more like a twelve-year-old than ever. She had been out in the sun and her freckles had gone a little crazy. Her red crew cut was standing straight up in the air. "You know how I'm going to finance all this?" she said. "This photography business?"

"How?"

"The minute I get out of high school, I'm going to get a scholarship to the New York Photography Institute. It's a two-year course. Then, when I'm really proficient, I'm going to run photo workshops. Have you ever seen them advertised in magazines? Yukon Adventures. Scottish Highlands Photo Workshop. Wilderness Workshops, East Africa Photography. You name it, they've got it. People pay a lot of money to go on a photo tour with an instructor. . . . I've even got the name of my outfit. Wild Horizons."

"In other words, that's how you'll buy your equipment."

"Exactly. I mean, hell, Woodruff, a person has got to hustle in this world. Nobody gives you anything."

"You have your whole life figured out. It's incredible."

"Well, not really, because something is bound to go wrong. As usual. But the basic idea is intelligent, if I do say so myself."

For a moment I couldn't think of anything to say. Because Mitzi Gerrard was so far ahead of me. It wasn't just that she was a year older. It was that she had done so much thinking about the future. "Tell me about that writer," I said. "Garret Smith."

She looked surprised. "Why do you mention him?"

"I don't know. It's just that when you talked about him the other day, your voice changed."

A shadow seemed to fall across her face. "I don't know what to tell you—but of all my mother's boyfriends, he was the best. I mean, he was good to me as well as to her, which is sort of unusual. Garret is a very educated person, and so he started me reading. The most fiction I had ever read in my life was the Nancy Drew books, but he started giving me real literature and all of a sudden I was reading people like H. D. Thoreau. I liked Garret so much that I even hoped my mother would marry him. But then he couldn't pay back that loan, and so they had an argument and broke up. It was a loss to me."

She sat there staring into space, and suddenly I felt very badly for her. Because I realized that this Garret Smith had been a father figure. "Who are your favorite authors?" I asked.

"Isak Dinesen and Jack London. People like that."

She lay down on the floor, and for a while there was silence between us. It wasn't a bad silence, just a pause between two friends. "Do you feel like talking about your brother?" she asked. "The one who's gay?"

"I don't know."

"I guess it must seem complicated to you."

"It does. That's the problem."

But before I knew it, I was talking about it— telling her everything that had happened since that night, two years ago, when Father had opened a letter to Cameron written by someone named David. I told her how close Cameron and I had been, and how lonely I was now. I couldn't believe I was doing it, but I was telling her everything. For the first time in my life, I was confiding in another human being.

When I paused for breath, Mitzi went over and opened the window. The room was filled with cigaret smoke. "You know, Woodruff, the way people give advice is usually this. You tell them your problem, and then they tell you it's not as bad as you think. They try to comfort you by saying that things are really not that bad. But usually they *are* that bad—so I'm not going to say that you're not suffering. But for the life of me, I don't know why you are looking at your brother's gayness as being a drawback. Maybe for him, it's an advantage."

"*What?*" I said.

"My mom has lots of gay friends, and I don't think any of them would want to change. They're happy. And gay people are just like everyone else, except in their sex life, so where's the big deal? The thing that's bothering you is not his gayness. It's that you miss him."

I was dumbstruck by this statement. Because the minute she said it, I knew it was true. My problem wasn't that Cameron was gay. It was that he loved Vincent now instead of me.

As though she were reading my mind, Mitzi said, "You probably feel like your brother doesn't love you anymore. Because he's got Vincent. But I'll tell you something, kid. If he loved you then, he loves you now. I mean, why would he change?"

"But he's never available anymore! It's like he's gone to the moon."

"He's in love, Woodruff. And people who are in love are like people who have the flu. They get sick for a while, and then they recover."

At that moment, Mitzi's mother opened the door. Without knocking. "Hey," she said, "don't you kids want to hear some music? Morton's playing the tapes he made in New Delhi."

"We're talking, Mom," said Mitzi.

"Well, OK, but can the cigarets. I can smell the smoke in the living room."

"Did you take your pill?" Mitzi asked her.

"Not yet," said Mrs. Gerrard.

"Mom," Mitzi said warningly.

Shirley Gerrard laughed. "OK, sweetheart, OK. . . . What would I do without her?" she said to me. And then she left the room.

"She's got high blood pressure," Mitzi explained. "She takes these pills."

"I guess I should be going," I said. "It's getting late."

"OK. If you must."

But the thought that we were going to leave it that way almost killed me. I mean, I just couldn't bear the thought of not seeing her tomorrow. And the day after that. And forever.

"Would you let me buy you a new camera?" I said. "A Nikon."

She looked startled. "Absolutely not."

"I've got some money in the bank. Quite a bit, actually."

"Woodruff, you're a character. I don't know

what to make of you."

"It would make me happy if I could buy you something."

She shook her head. "No way. But I appreciate the thought."

And then Mitzi Gerrard did an amazing thing. She got to her feet, and came over to me, and kissed me. On the cheek. "Call me tomorrow," she said.

SEVENTEEN

What would have happened to me if I hadn't met Mitzi Gerrard? It's difficult to know what my fate would have been, but I'll tell you this much— she saved me. Without even knowing what she was saving me *from*, I had this feeling that I was a drowning man being rescued. It's like that poem that Mitzi recited to me once, by a woman named Stevie Smith. "I was much further out than you thought," the poem goes, "And not waving but drowning."

We did everything together, seven days a week, and here's how it worked. In the mornings, we would meet by the pond at dawn and take pictures. Then we would part until lunchtime, since

Mitzi had to work at her mother's store. At noon we would meet at Olsen's, where we usually had a sandwich together, and then we would part again while Mitzi put in her hours there. By dinnertime we were together again, usually at her place, and on Saturdays I hung around the car wash while she worked. Sunday was the one free day we had, and we always made the most of it by taking our cameras and our bikes and heading for someplace remote. The wildlife refuge over on Shelter Island, or the ocean beach. I began to get used to Mitzi's mother, and to Morton the faith healer, and I even began to help out at Mustard Seed on Thursday evenings. More about that later.

Mitzi Gerrard may only have been fifteen, but she knew more about nature than most people at forty. I was amazed by her fund of knowledge, considering that she had grown up in cities. She and her mother had lived all over the country, from Seattle to New York, and Mitzi had been independent from the time she was seven—learning to beat up any kid on the block, as she put it. When she was twelve she and her mother had come out to The Hamptons because of some guy Mrs. Gerrard was involved with, and they had liked it and stayed. What else can I tell you about Mitzi? That she had won a breakdancing contest once, in the East Village, and that she was a terrific roller skater. In addition to which, she was the only teenager I had ever met (except me) whose life was not consumed by rock music. I am very aware that rock is the strongest force on earth right now, but it didn't touch Mitzi at all. If anything, she liked to listen to Brahms and Grieg, and people like that. Nor, of course, did she do drugs. Where she wanted to be was out in the wilderness. "I'll be in East Africa before I'm twenty-one," she was fond of saying. "Where the big game is."

Not that I understood her. I had never had a friend, much less a female one, so there were plenty of things about her that baffled me. Like the fact that she had a private streak of sentimentality. Once, when her wallet was lying open on a table, I saw a picture of a man in it—who I assumed to be Garret—and sometimes, when I least expected her to, she would quote long passages from Stevie Smith. "She lived her whole life with an aunt," Mitzi said to me, "an elderly aunt. And never got married. She worked in an office and had a very dull life, and died of a brain tumor. What do you think of that?"

Meanwhile, my life at home was in abeyance, if that is the right word. I checked in and out, and mowed the lawn, and kept looking for Zeppo (who had been missing for weeks now), but it was almost like I didn't live there anymore. Father didn't particularly notice, but Mother was confused. "Who *is* this little girl?" she kept asking. "Who are her people?" Briefly, I would consider having Mitzi and her mother over to tea or something, and then I would dismiss the thought. Shirley Gerrard and my mother would definitely not mix. On the other hand, Mother was so surprised that I had a friend that she tried to keep quiet about it most of the time—which I appreciated.

All of which brings me to Cameron. He and Vincent were in Europe now, for a month's vacation, and not a day passed that we didn't get postcards. Postcards from Vienna, from Zurich, from Florence, and God knows where else. I didn't even read these postcards, just glanced at the pictures on them. Because Cameron was gone as far as I was concerned. Gone from my life and my heart. His photo was no longer on my bureau and I had thrown all his letters away—the ones he used to write me when I was at camp.

This thing that is called "the season" had descended on The Hamptons—and The Hamptons in July and August is a very odd place. Incredible vintage cars roll through the streets of the towns, and you are apt to bump into celebrities in the hardware store. People work on their tans, and go to cocktail parties and gallery openings—and in the midst of the whole thing, the wildlife try to survive. That was the part I always found so strange. The fact that this crazy human civilization was going on—with cars and beach parties and kids on motorbikes—while just a few feet away would be a swan with a cygnet, hidden in the tall grass.

Every Thursday evening Mrs. Gerrard had a meeting of her Past Lives group, which was a group of people who firmly believed that they had lived before. In the Middle Ages or the 18th century. In early Rome. And while this group was meeting at the Gerrards' apartment, Mitzi and I would run the store, which was open on Thursdays till 9:00 p.m. Mother was amazed that I was working in such a place, but then she decided that it was probably a healthy environment. (Unlike a movie house or a disco.) What I didn't tell her, of course, was that I was working for free.

At first, the atmosphere at Mustard Seed made me nervous. But the kind of people who came into the place, to buy things like Spirulina or Evening Primrose Oil, interested me because they were all what Father would call "fringe." In other words, they were weird. There were massage therapists and weight counselors, people who did grief counseling, and two women who told me that they were witches. And of course, there was always

Morton the faith healer, getting his meals for free and taking anything he wanted from the shelves. Bottles of vitamins, bags of sunflower seeds. The only word Morton ever said to me was "Hey," or "Hey, man," making me wonder if he was retarded. "No, no," Mitzi assured me. "He's just inarticulate." Morton lived in an abandoned chapel on Shelter Island, where he saw his clients. Sick and crippled people came to him for healing sessions, and sometimes, Mitzi told me, the sessions worked.

The thing that bothered me was the fact that Morton and Mrs. Gerrard took advantage of Mitzi. If there was some stupid errand to be done, it was always Mitzi who did it, and she also cooked for the three of them and did the grocery shopping. Morton had an elderly dog named Homer, whom he never took care of, and so Homer became Mitzi's responsibility. Flea baths, vitamins, trips to the vet. It drove me wild. "Can't you see she's taking advantage of you?" I said once. But Mitzi just looked baffled. "I don't know what you're talking about, Woodruff. She's my *mother*."

Another thing that concerned me was the way Mitzi ate. Like a Japanese wrestler. Two and three hamburgers at a time, and—at Olsen's—all the ice cream she wanted. But one day she told me that she and Mrs. Gerrard had gone hungry in the old days, after her father had left. "We lived on generic peanut butter and day-old bread," Mitzi explained. "And a lot of times we stole things from supermarkets." People had urged Mrs. Gerrard to put Mitzi up for adoption—that's how poor they were—but, to her credit, Mrs. Gerrard hadn't done that. Instead, she had worked on raising the capital for all these health food places.

Sag Harbor had been turned upside down because of the movie that was being made. It was a film about the American Revolution, and entire battles were being staged in people's backyards. I'm not a movie buff, so I didn't recognize any of the actors in this film, but Mother took her little Instamatic camera and joined the crowd that watched every day from the sidelines. Alan Roberts was directing and starring, and she had a big crush on him. And I cannot tell you why, but something about Mother hurrying to town every day, to watch Alan Roberts direct the same scene over and over, saddened me. She even sent a picture of him she had taken to the local paper, hoping that they would publish it.

Mitzi wasn't interested in the movie either. All she cared about was having enough time to spend in the woods or down by the pond. Every bird in The Hamptons, it seemed, had had its young (all except Zeppo, who was still missing) and Mitzi and I were going through masses of film, trying to photograph the whole thing. There were ducklings, and Canada goslings, and most of all there was the cygnet on Fresh Pond. You could see now that he was going to be a swan, because his baby looks had disappeared and his neck was slender and long. Mitzi had dozens of pictures of him, showing his development from the day he had hatched, and I had named him Arnold—because of his fondness for Arnold bread. Silly and anthropomorphic, I guess, but that's me.

EIGHTEEN

It was a hot July day, and Mitzi and I were sitting
on one of the small cliffs that overhang the North
Haven beach. North Haven is not exactly famous
for cliffs, but the two of us had found this pro-
montory and were having a picnic there. Mitzi
had already eaten two sandwiches and a bag of
cookies, and now she was staring at the bay
through her binoculars. "Look quickly!" she said.
"I think I see a flock of ibis." Well, by the time
I had focused my binoculars they were gone—
just some black shapes in the distance. "Missed
them," I said.

"Yep," said Mitzi, "they were glossy ibis, all
right. An odd-looking bird."

"What's their range?"

"They come down from Maine and fly along the Atlantic to the Gulf Coast. Then they wind up near Texas."

"Have you ever wondered why birds migrate?"

She gave me a sharp look. "Wonder? It is one of my main preoccupations. I think about it all the time."

"It's a survival tactic, I guess."

"Don't oversimplify. There are dozens of reasons for birds to migrate, and scientists still don't know the whole story. . . . Do you know where I wish I was? At this very moment?"

"Where?" I asked.

Mitzi lay flat on her back and gazed up at the sky. "On the Serengeti Plain, stalking lions. The first place I want to go, when I'm a professional, is the Serengeti—and the second place is the Himalayas. After that, I'm going to the rain forest of Borneo."

"It's a great life, photography."

"It is also a hard life. A lot of nature photographers burn themselves out. Or get tropical diseases."

I lay down next to her and stared at the clouds. "Which is why you should stop smoking."

"I'll stop, I'll stop. Just don't bug me about it."

A big cloud passed by in the shape of a horse.

"Do you think they'll drop the bomb?" I said. "Someday?"

"Yes," she said. "I do."

I was surprised that she had said this. "Then what's the point?"

"Of what?"

"Of everything."

Mitzi sighed. "What you're asking me is why we should care about nature if it's all going to blow up. My answer to you is the same thing the man said about climbing the mountain. Because it's there."

I don't know what made me do it, but I reached over and took her hand. She let me hold it for a moment, then she pulled away. "I'm sorry. I can't hold hands right now."

I felt very embarrassed. "I'm sorry. I didn't mean to do that."

"It's all right. You have every right to hold my goddam hand if you want to. It's just that physical things turn me off these days."

I wasn't sure what she was talking about, but I said, "Sure."

There was a pause, and then she said, "This guy—one of my mother's friends, actually—tried to mess around with me last year."

"How do you mean? Sexually?"

She gave a bitter laugh. "Well, it wasn't spiritu-

141

ally, I'll tell you that much. He got me alone in the apartment one night, when my mother was away, and tried to mess around."

"God. I'm sorry."

"I fought him off so hard that he's probably a cripple by now. I kicked him in the groin, and then I used a few of my karate chops. I also pulled out some of his hair."

"He tried to rape you?"

"More or less," she said calmly. "But I leveled the bastard. He'll never be the same again."

"Did you ever tell her? Your mother?"

"No, she has enough on her mind. I mean, why would I worry her with something so stupid? The bastard stopped hanging around our place, that's all. He split."

The idea that anyone had tried to rape Mitzi Gerrard depressed me into my very bones. I mean, she was so little, compared to most grown men. "I'm sorry I took your hand," I said to her. "I didn't know."

Mitzi flipped over on her stomach and began to fumble around for her cigarets. "That's OK, kid. Actually, I like you very much."

"You do?"

"Yeah, I do. You've got a good heart."

She found one of her cigarets, lit it, and blew a big smoke ring. "Which is why you should forgive that brother of yours."

"I don't know what you mean."

"Oh, yes you do, Woodruff. You've decided to cut that poor guy right out of your life, simply because of Vincent. You want to pay him back for being in love."

"Not necessarily."

"Retribution is a crummy thing. And also, there's something you haven't considered—which is that your brother has guts."

I stared at her. "How do you mean?"

"It takes courage to be gay these days, Woodruff. With the kind of backlash that's going on and everything. I mean, your brother didn't have to come out of the closet and open himself to all kinds of ridicule. But he did, and that takes guts."

I didn't want to talk about Cameron at all. Not one word. So to change the subject, I said, "Do you know what I did last week?"

Mitzi was studying a small seashell, turning it over in her hand. "What?"

"I wrote Mr. Olsen a letter about that ice-cream contest."

"Jesus," she said. "Aren't you over that yet? That was weeks ago. How can you bear such a grudge?"

"It isn't a grudge."

"Oh, yes it is."

"Crazy Vanilla is better than Pineapple Pothole. I know it, and you know it. There's no comparison."

"So what? So the hell what? If life were *fair*, kid, I wouldn't be sitting here with you. I'd be in East Africa, where the big game is. If life were fair, I'd have a Nikon instead of that sad little Kodak I'm using—and if life were fair, that bastard, whose name, by the way, is Harold J. Sloanburg, would be behind bars for attempted rape. But since life is *not* fair, why don't you just forgive Mr. Olsen for being dense and get on with things?"

"I can't take an attitude like that."

Mitzi sat up and ran a hand through her hair. "Well, I'll tell you something. If you don't learn to take that attitude, you'll always be in trouble. Always be blaming someone else for the things that happen. I mean—God!—I've had to accept a lot of things in my life. Like Harold J. Sloanburg, and like losing Garret. Garret Smith was the best friend I've ever had, but he left us. So now, with the exception of my mother, who thinks I'm demented, I'm alone in the world. So what? I'll manage. I'll survive."

"I . . . I know this doesn't sound like much,"

I said to her. "But you have me now. If that's any comfort."

Her mouth twitched a little, and she looked away. Out over the water, toward Jessup Neck. "Thank you," she said.

"You're welcome," I replied.

She gave a little snort. "That stupid Harold J. Sloanburg. I really leveled him."

"Should we go back now? It's getting sort of late."

"Yeah, let's go back. The idyll is over."

"What's an idyll?" I asked, as we packed up our picnic things.

Mitzi grinned at me. "Look it up in the dictionary."

NINETEEN

Mother was sitting at the kitchen table, studying the snapshots she had taken of Alan Roberts. All of which I found very ironic. My mother the photographer. "Which one of these do you like?" she asked. "You're the expert."

I looked at the pictures. Alan Roberts in blue jeans. Alan Roberts in costume. Alan Roberts talking through a megaphone, waving his arms, lighting a cigaret. I couldn't see anything special about him, but it was clear that Mother thought he was great. "I don't know," I said. "They're all good."

"He is the most interesting young man. And so deeply talented. I just love watching him work."

"But they do the same scenes over and over,

Mom. Don't you find it boring?"

"Oh, my goodness no," said Mother. "Certainly not."

I remembered that Mother had wanted to be an actress once. When she was in her teens. "I bet you'd like to be in the movie with him," I said to her.

To my surprise, she blushed. "Why honey, that's the silliest thing I've ever heard."

But I could tell that it was true, and somehow this made me realize, for the thousandth time, that most people never get what they want out of life. Mother had wanted to be an actress when she was young, and Father had wanted to be a doctor (until Grandfather Woodruff insisted that he become a stockbroker) and Cameron had had to fight like hell just to be a designer, and I—if I was going to make it at all—would have to stage some kind of minor revolution to become a photographer. The only person I knew who was sure to get what she wanted was Mitzi. Nothing would stop her, because she didn't believe in obstacles.

Mother was still talking about Alan Roberts, but my thoughts were far away—back on that little cliff where I had taken Mitzi's hand. If I had told anyone at school that I had recently held a girl's hand, for the first time, for around two minutes, they would have broken up. I mean, the way people make out in my school is fantastic, and many of the girls are on birth control pills. But to me, holding Mitzi Gerrard's hand had been a deeply moving experience, and I wondered if it would ever happen again. It was crazy that I had found her homely at first, because now I found her beautiful. Sometimes when she watched Arnold the swan, down at the pond, there would be a gentle look on her face, a look she wasn't aware of, and I couldn't take my eyes off her. I knew she was short, and had a snub nose, and a crew cut, but she was beautiful to me all the same.

"He's using three hundred extras," Mother was saying. "And all of them local people."

"No kidding," I said. But my mind had drifted away again, this time to Cameron and the letter I had received from him. The letter was from the Swiss Alps, where he and Vincent were hiking, and while I don't want to bore you by quoting all of it, this is how the last paragraph went:

We'll be home in ten days, old buddy, and I'm really looking forward to seeing you. All through this trip I've been wishing you were with us, to share the fantastic things we've seen. Vincent really likes you, you know, and I think he's a little hurt that you haven't been friendlier. I miss you, Tyler, and miss the kind of talks we used to have.

Remember how we used to talk together far into the night, at the New York apartment? I always felt you were ten years old going on forty, you were such a good friend to me. All for now.

Love,
Cameron.

Reading this letter had been so painful that I had folded it up, very quickly, and put it at the bottom of my socks-and-clean-underwear drawer. Yet if you had asked me why it was painful, I couldn't have told you.

"Stacy Parish tried out for the movie, but didn't get a part," Mother was saying. "Which is just amazing, really, when you consider what a beauty she is."

I was opening my mouth to reply, when Zeppo walked into the yard.

There had been some quacking in the distance that I hadn't paid attention to. But now I rose to my feet and went over to the kitchen door. Zeppo and six ducklings were hurrying across the grass, single file, towards the birdseed. She had had her babies and they were the size of dandelions.

"Zeppo's back," I said to Mother. "I've got to get the camera." And, while Mother stood at the kitchen door saying things like, "Isn't that the most cunning thing you have ever *seen*?" I began clicking away. Zeppo and her young were attacking the birdseed on the ground like they hadn't eaten for days. Then all of the ducklings jumped into the water dish and began to swim.

Like all little mallards, they were black with gold stripes, and very active. I went through one roll of film, and put in another. I got down on my knees in the backyard and moved slowly towards the ducklings, talking softly to Zeppo, who was nervous about sharing them with me. I finished the second roll of film, and knew that I had gotten some very good pictures. But Zeppo was apprehensive. With a commanding quack she led the ducklings away, single file, down to the cove.

I sat on the kitchen steps, wondering if this was Zeppo's first brood of the summer, or her second. They often have two. Then, with a certain amount of surprise, I realized something. For the first time since I had met Zeppo, a year ago, I had reacted to her with dispassion.

TWENTY

The summer went by so quickly that we were in the middle of August before I realized it. Father had spent his two-week vacation with us, but hadn't really enjoyed it because he never knows what to do with himself when he is in North Haven. He putters around the garden, and walks down to the cove twice a day, but away from New York City he is rather lost. Mother kept driving into town, to watch the movie being made, and Mitzi and I kept trying to coordinate our schedules. The fact that school would be starting in a few weeks depressed me—because it would put Mitzi and me into different worlds. The kids at Peterson High are very tough, and often drop out when they are sixteen to start work. Whereas the kids at my school sometimes arrive in chauffered cars in the morning and have their birthday parties at country clubs. All of which offends me.

Cameron had arrived back from Europe—though none of us had seen him. He and Vincent were working nine and ten hours a day, and on weekends they just rested or went to the movies. The first time Cameron had called, to say he was back, he had seemed terribly glad to talk to me—but I had been cold as ice. I wanted to be friendlier, but couldn't. Don't ask me why.

All through August I had the feeling that something terrible was about to happen. Something disastrous. This feeling would wake me in the middle of the night, or come over me when I was mowing lawns, and I couldn't seem to shake it. Maybe I felt that my friendship with Mitzi was too good to be true, or maybe I was simply going through "changes," as Mrs. Gerrard calls them. At any rate, I felt like I was living on borrowed time. Finally, I told Mitzi about it, but she just shook her head. "It's all in your imagination, Woodruff. Just ignore it."

It was five-thirty in the morning and we were sitting by the pond, watching Arnold—who was now a very big bird, though still pearl-gray. He sailed through the early light with a parent on either side of him, looking plump and well-fed. But why shouldn't he have been well-fed? I gave him half a loaf of Arnold bread every day.

"I get those feelings very often," Mitzi continued. "Feelings of doom. But I just tell them to bugger off."

I was putting film into my camera. "And does that work?"

"Sometimes. Sometimes not."

It wasn't light enough to photograph yet, so we just sat there watching the sun rise over Sag Harbor. Arnold was eating his bread and the swan parents were circling him. Slowly, watchfully.

"It's like that poem you recited to me once," I said to Mitzi. " 'I was much further out than you thought And not waving but drowning.' "

Mitzi patted my shoulder. "You're not drowning, kid. Waving maybe, but not drowning."

"I keep feeling that something awful is about to happen."

"It isn't."

"Like I had cancer or something."

"You don't. And speaking of cancer, have you noticed anything today? About me?"

I looked at her carefully. Bare feet, faded jeans, and a pajama top on under a cotton Windbreaker. "You're not smoking," I said.

"You got it, Woodruff. I kicked the habit."

"Fantastic! When did that happen?"

"Yesterday. At two in the afternoon."

"Hurray," I said. Without thinking, I hugged her.

Her first reaction was to pull back, but then she allowed me to hug her—very briefly. "How do you feel without cigarets?" I asked.

"Like hell. I'm having withdrawal."

"I wonder what you could do about that."

"I don't know. Eat, I guess. Which I do anyway."

"The light is starting," I said. Which sounded odd, but Mitzi knew what I meant. She began to focus her camera.

And once again, for the hundredth time, I wished that I had won that ice-cream contest. The sight of Mitzi Gerrard—the best photographer I knew—working with a Kodak she had bought at the thrift shop made me feel wild. But there was nothing I could do about it.

The rising sun had made a path of gold across the water, and Arnold the swan was swimming lazily across it. He had finished his bread and was about to leave, his parents still in attendance. I focused my zoom and shot five or six pictures. Mitzi did the same.

It was terribly quiet, no sounds at all except for an owl somewhere who still thought it was night. Snowy egrets were running back and forth

154

in the shallows, fishing. On a rock in the middle of the pond was a little blue heron.

"Arnold has gotten so huge," I said.

Mitzi laughed softly. "It kills me the way you have to name everything. Arnold the swan. Zeppo the duck."

"I'm getting better about all that."

"It's true. You are."

I took her hand, and she didn't pull away. And suddenly I realized that I loved her. It had taken all these days, all these weeks, to realize this.

"Recite that poem for me," I said. "The one about waving and drowning."

"On a nice morning like this? With everything so peaceful?"

"Sure. Why not?"

Mitzi frowned and gazed across the pond. "OK, But I wish I had a cigaret."

> Nobody heard him, the dead man,
> But still he lay moaning:
> I was much further out than you thought
> And not waving but drowning.
>
> Poor chap, he always loved larking
> And now he's dead
> It must have been too cold for him his
>   heart gave way,
> They said.

155

Oh, no no no, it was too cold always
(Still the dead one lay moaning)
I was much too far out all my life
And not waving but drowning.

"That's a great poem," I said.

"I know."

"But I'll be damned how you can remember all that stuff. Poems, quotations."

"It was Garret who started me doing that. Memorizing. Garret Smith knew more poems by heart than you could shake a stick at. He could also quote Shakespeare."

We were still holding hands, and my own was getting sweaty. Which worried me. "Do you still miss him?" I asked.

Mitzi took her hand away. "Not so much anymore."

"Were you in love with him?"

"Maybe. I don't know. At times he seemed like a father to me, and then at other times . . . I just don't know."

"I saw his picture in your wallet once."

She looked surprised. "You did?"

"Yeah. By accident."

"I'll keep it there always," she said. "For the rest of my life."

The swans had disappeared into the sunlight.

And dozens of birds were singing. "Do you remember the first time we met?" she asked. "Down here by the pond?"

"Sure."

"You told me you were on assignment for a magazine."

"I know. I was lying."

"That was obvious. But I wondered why you had to lie."

"I don't know. To impress you, I guess."

"You didn't have to do that—I was already impressed."

I stared at her. "You were?"

"Sure. You're a very good-looking guy, Woodruff, though you don't seem to be aware of it. And you had all that camera gear with you. And bossy! I thought you were the bossiest person I'd ever met."

I laughed. "I felt the same way about you."

"What are we going to do about school starting?" she asked. "How are we going to see each other?"

"I don't know. The thought of the whole thing drives me crazy."

"We won't have any spare time together."

"I know."

She sighed. "If I didn't have certain responsibilities, I'd suggest that we split."

"How do you mean?"

"Hit the road. Take off. But I simply can't do that as long as my mother needs me. She depends on me for everything."

"That stinks!" I said. "It really does."

"It may or may not stink, but that's how it is. I have to go to work now, Woodruff. It's getting late."

"We're always saying good-bye," I said to her.

"And also, hello," she replied.

TWENTY-ONE

My school was supposed to open on September 9th, and Mitzi's a few days later. And whereas you might think I felt excited about starting high school, the only thing in my mind was how Mitzi and I were going to see each other. She had given up her jobs at Olsen's and the car wash, but she still worked at Mustard Seed, and she had elected to take some extra courses this year—like carpentry and auto repair. I was taking difficult subjects like algebra and German and "Understanding Computers"—and when I realized how complicated all this was going to be, I almost despaired. Anyway, on September 9th I became a freshman in high school. As usual, nobody talked to me the first day, except one kid who wanted to know where the boys' bathroom was. And my German teacher persisted in calling me Skylar. So my first days of high school (prep school, to be exact) were not exactly sublime.

Something had happened at home, however, that had significance to me—and this concerned Father. All summer Mitzi had been urging me to frame my pictures and put them up on the wall, and so I finally framed an 8 × 12 enlargement of Zeppo and hung it in the living room. Not my bedroom, mind you, the living room—where everyone would be sure to see it. It was a portrait of Zeppo done before she had become a mother, and she was sitting down near the cove gazing at the water. It was sunset, and the light was striking her in a very interesting way. As I have told you before, there are times when Zeppo looks more intelligent than she is, and this was one of those times.

At any rate, it was the weekend after I had started high school, and Mother, Father and I were sitting in the living room having dinner on little tables and watching the television news. Suddenly Father looked at the wall near the fireplace and said, "What's *that*?"

"What's what?" I said innocently.

"That picture," he said. "That bird."

Mother jumped into the situation, hoping to deflect it. (If that's the right word.) "Why sweetheart, that is one of Tyler's photos. Isn't it lovely?"

"It's a duck," said Father. "As a matter of fact, it's the same goddam duck that used to follow me around the lawn."

"Her name is Zeppo," I said. "After the Marx Brothers."

Father looked at me, and then he looked at the photo. "Tyler, I don't really want that hanging in the living room. It looks peculiar."

"I'd like it to stay."

Well, in all the fourteen years I had been on this earth, I had never said such a thing to Father. Never asserted myself, never contradicted him, never stood up for what I wanted. And so he was startled.

"Georgie, where's the harm?" said Mother. "It's only a picture."

"I do not want it in the living room. Is that clear?"

"I live here too," I said. "And I'd like it to stay."

He looked at me sharply. "Do you pay the bills?"

"No—but I mow the lawn, and wax your car, and clip the hedge, and do a million other things that you never even thank me for. So if I want to put one of my photos on the wall, I think you should let me."

"Now, listen here . . ."

"I'm going to be a very good photographer," I said, "and you don't even know it. That's the crazy part—that you don't even know I have talent. Mother knows it, and Cameron, and my friend Mitzi. But you treat me like I'm invisible. If I had two talented children, one of whom is a designer and the other of whom is a photographer, I'd be *proud*. But you know something, Father? You're just so involved in yourself that you don't even know we exist."

Father's mouth had dropped open. As for Mother, she looked frightened. Father has a terrible temper—I mean, he once took an entire Christmas tree and threw it out the window during an argument—and we have all spent our lives being afraid of him. But I wasn't afraid any longer, because I didn't give a damn.

The photo of Zeppo stayed on the wall and nothing more was said about it. So I framed a few other enlargements—of swans—and Mother and I hung them in selected areas around the house. Father pretended that the whole thing had never happened, but sometimes, on weekends, I would see him gazing at me. As though he were seeing me for the first time. I wish I could say I was pleased about this, but in some ways I felt it was too late. I should have spoken up to him long ago—when I was little.

Cameron had come down to Long Island just once, in August, but I hadn't been home. It was a Sunday, and Mitzi and I had made plans to photograph an osprey's nest that had been mentioned in the local paper. There were two chicks in the nest, and a lot of photographers had taken pictures—from a safe distance—and we wanted to do the same. So when Cameron and Vincent had come for Sunday lunch, I hadn't been there. "Your brother was just so disappointed to have missed you," Mother said to me that night. "He couldn't understand your absence."

"I had a date with Mitzi. It was important."

"Well honey," Mother said dubiously, "I guess it was."

I looked at Mother, aware of how much she had had to drink that day, and aware of how awful she would feel the next morning, and wondered if I would ever have the courage to do something Mitzi had suggested. Which was to take Mother to Alcoholics Anonymous. "Your mom has a real problem," Mitzi had said, "but AA might work for her. I mean, she likes people, and AA is very friendly and social." So I had looked up AA in the phone book and had asked them to send me some literature, which they did and which I read with a sinking heart. Because Mother fit all their descriptions of alcoholism. A few days later, when she was out shopping, I put the literature on her bureau. I felt disloyal for doing this, but deep down I knew it was the right thing.

The month of September was frantic, and both Mitzi and I felt like we were living three lives apiece. There was school, and homework, and photography, and there was also Mustard Seed and my job with Mrs. Edgeworth. You may not believe this, but one day I missed Mitzi so much that I simply walked out of school, boarded a bus, and got off at Peterson High, which is just outside Sag Harbor. It was lunchtime and I spotted Mitzi at once—standing in the parking lot with her camera. She was photographing an old dog who was sleeping near some cars, and her concentration was so great that she could have been a million miles away. I didn't speak to her or anything, just stood and watched her—and the more I contemplated her, the more I realized what a loner she was. Everywhere you looked there were groups of kids—talking, smoking, horsing around—but Mitzi Gerrard wasn't connected to any of them. She was more of a loner than I was, and all the way back to Southampton on the bus I thought about this.

I began to dream about Mitzi every night. Either

we were in Africa together, or Iceland, or the Galá-pagos, and there was always some great adventure just ahead of us. We never seemed to reach the great adventure—but there was a feeling of tremendous happiness in these dreams. One night I even dreamed that I married her, on a riverbank in the Serengeti—and that one woke me up. I could hear the TV playing downstairs (Mother watching a late movie) but otherwise the house was still.

TWENTY-TWO

Ask yourself what being in love means to different people, and you'll get some very strange answers. There is a kid in my class who is in love with his pet loggerhead turtle, and I have always felt that Father was in love with his car. Cameron, of course, is in love with Vincent—and all last summer Mother seemed to be in love with Alan Roberts, whom she didn't even know. Then there was the way I felt about Mitzi. As though she had changed the world for me. As though she had taken an invisible paintbrush and colored everything beautiful. I was seeing things with her that I had never seen before, never noticed, and the closer we got, the more I realized that she was what Cameron would call "an old soul." In other words, she had been born wise. I could never really tell if she loved me back—though I think she did—but much of the time it didn't matter because we had such harmony together. Each of us knew what the other was thinking so often that it got to be a joke. "Did you bring the . . ." she would start to say, down at the pond. And without blinking an eye, I would say, "Yeah, the tripod. It's on the back of my bike."

This being such an oversexed world, you are probably wondering if I wanted to make out with Mitzi, if I ever thought about it. The answer is yes, I thought about it all the time, but somehow it never happened. Does it matter if you make out with the person you love, or merely hold their hand? Does the love you feel for them change according to how physical you get? These questions are still unanswered for me, and it isn't just because I'm young. It's because they are hard questions.

One morning the phone was ringing at 5:00 a.m. in the downstairs hall. Fortunately, it was I who woke up and not Mother. I ran down the stairs and grabbed the phone on its fifth ring. "Woodruff," said Mitzi's voice. "I need to see you."

I rubbed the sleep out of my eyes. "What's wrong?" I asked. "Is anything wrong?"

"Something has happened."

"I'll be at the pond in ten minutes. No, make it fifteen. I need a cup of coffee. Can you tell me what it is?"

"I need to see you in person."

"I'll be there. And Mitzi?"

"Yes?"

"Nothing. I'll be there soon."

I went upstairs, stripped off my pajamas, pulled on jeans and a shirt, and hurried down to the kitchen—where I made a cup of instant coffee. I had a terrible feeling that someone had died, Mrs. Gerrard maybe, and in the pit of my stomach I was shaking. I had never heard Mitzi sound that way.

I got my bike from the garage, and in ten minutes I had reached the pond. There was a new smell in the air—of autumn—and leaves were falling. It was only the end of September, but everything had changed.

As a dull copper light came into the sky, I looked around for the swans. Nothing, no one, just a mallard duck standing in the shallows. I heard Mitzi's bike approaching on the pond road. You could always hear it coming because it was such a wreck.

Footsteps were sounding in the dry leaves, and then she was beside me—wearing an old raincoat over her pajamas, her hair standing on end. She looked terrible, like she hadn't slept all night.

"What is it?" I said. "What happened?"

She took a cigaret out of her pocket and fumbled around for a match.

"You're smoking," I said.

"I know. Don't bug me about it."

We both sat down on the little beach, and I waited for her to speak. Whatever was wrong, I knew I couldn't push her to tell me about it. You couldn't push Mitzi to do anything. You had to wait until she was ready. I began to pray that her mother hadn't died. God, I said silently, please don't let anyone be dead.

"We're moving," she said at last. "To Santa Fe, New Mexico. In three weeks."

I stared at her without the slightest comprehension. "I don't know what you're talking about."

"My mother and Morton . . . they've decided to move to New Mexico, where Morton's cousin has started a Wellness Center. My mother's friend Edith is taking over the store. The lease, the merchandise, everything."

"I don't believe it."

"It's true. We're leaving."

She was on her second cigaret now, but she hadn't looked at me. She just couldn't bring herself to do it, so she stared at the water and at the swans—who had suddenly appeared. I hadn't brought any bread for them.

"Look how big Arnold is," she said.

"Mitzi . . ."

"Don't make it hard for me, Woodruff. There's nothing I can do. I'm only fifteen."

"We could run away. We could—"

"My mother needs me. Where she goes, I go too."

"*Why?*"

"Because she's my mother, dammit!"

I wanted to sound forceful, but when my voice did come out, it was more like a sob. "But what about me?"

"I don't know. I don't know anything anymore. God! No sooner do we get settled in one place than we take off for another. I was beginning to like it here. I really was."

"I'll come with you."

"That's impossible."

"I won't let you go."

She looked at me for the first time, and I could see the pain in her eyes. "I won't let you go," I said. "You're my friend."

But it wasn't what I wanted to say at all. What I wanted to say was that I loved her and that I would never love anyone else. What I wanted to say was that because of her I had started to see the whole world differently. I wanted to tell her how beautiful she was, and how special, and how totally unlike anyone else. And I also wanted to tell her how much I admired her. But do you know something? I didn't say any of that, not a single word.

"It isn't fair," I said after a while.

"When was it ever?" she replied, putting her cigarets into the pocket of her coat. "I have to go now. I have to get ready for school."

"Don't go yet. Please."

"OK," she said.

"You'll be leaving in the middle of the school year."

"Sure. Of course."

"That's kind of rough."

She got to her feet and ran one hand through her crew cut. "It's autumn," she said. "In a few months, Arnold will be grown."

I gazed out over the pond. "When will he start to fly?"

"Pretty soon. Then the parents will drive him away and he'll be on his own for a while. Until he finds a mate. Then he and his mate will have their own family, and so it goes."

I touched her arm. "Can I pick you up after school? Can we talk?"

She smiled at me, but it was the saddest smile I had ever seen. "Sure," she replied. "Be my guest."

TWENTY-THREE

It's funny, but the last weeks Mitzi and I had together were the best. I don't know whether it was because everything was coming to an end, or whether we had just grown closer, but before she left we had three weeks of perfect happiness. She had started cutting school, because Peterson High didn't matter to her now, and I typed a letter to the principal at Country-Day on my mother's stationery—saying that Tyler was having some very complicated dentistry at the moment and would have to miss a few classes.

I guess we were trying to live a lifetime in three weeks, Mitzi and I, because we did some very wonderful things. Like taking the bus to New York and seeing the Audubon show at a museum over on the West Side. (It was a rare experience, because these paintings aren't shown very often.) Or like going to every wildlife refuge in The Hamptons. We photographed everything, and now because it was autumn the great blue herons had re-turned—flying like gray shawls over the harbor, or standing motionless at dawn in the marshes.

And then there was Arnold, who was being taught to fly by his parents, and who had grown into a huge homely bird. He would be beautiful as an adult, but now, as a big adolescent, he looked awful. But the way his parents were teaching him to fly was terrific. They would rush across the pond, flapping their wings and calling back to him—in their odd snorting voices—to follow. And because of his anxiety at being left alone, he would hurry after them. Mitzi said that any day he would be airborne.

Whole days would pass when I felt all right, when I felt busy and normal. But then the knowl-edge that Mitzi would soon be leaving would wash over me and I would get so depressed I could hardly move. There were mornings when I felt so terrible I could hardly get out of bed, but I always did—pretending to go to school at seven-thirty, when most of the time I was heading to town, to meet Mitzi at a coffee shop. I knew that eventually there would be hell to pay about my cutting school. But I didn't care.

Mitzi didn't show much emotion during those weeks. When she wasn't with me, she was helping her mother wind up a million details at Mustard Seed. Edith Kervakian, who was taking over the business, was adding a lot of new items—like cookware—and was also planning on a sidewalk café in the summers. As for Morton, he did nothing to help anyone. As usual. The Gerrards were taking Morton's dog with them, and the two kittens as well. They would make the trip west in Morton's van.

I went to the local bookstore and bought some books on New Mexico. It looked like a wasteland to me. A lot of old towns with adobe buildings in them, and dusty streets, and a hard blue sky. It also looked arty—in the sense that there were all these little galleries and pottery shops. I don't know. Maybe if I had been going to New Mexico too, I could have gotten excited about it.

Meanwhile, Mother was still drinking (though I knew she had read that literature I put in her room, because it had disappeared from the bureau) and Father was still the same rigid person he had always been. Mitzi's interpretation of Father was that he was quite emotional underneath, but that he had been brought up not to show it, and that deep down he loved Cameron and me. Quite possibly this is true, and I will always give him the benefit of the doubt, but we still don't connect. All he ever asks me about these days is school, and what grades I am getting—which is an extremely boring topic.

The weekend arrived that the Gerrards were to leave—and my depression was so great that it frightened me. I mean, I thought about suicide and things like that. I also developed a stomachache that wouldn't go away. They were leaving early Sunday morning, so that Mitzi and I had decided to say good-bye on Saturday, down at the pond. For three weeks I had known what I was going to give her as a going-away gift, and so on Friday afternoon I went to a photo store in Southampton and bought a Nikon camera with a zoom lens, and a flash attachment, and a camera bag. This purchase took all of my savings, but I didn't care. I just wanted her to go off to New Mexico well equipped. It was a fantastic camera, if I do say so myself. State of the art. Lightweight. Compact.

Our last meeting was on October 13th down at the pond. We had agreed to meet there at dawn, to photograph Arnold for one last time, but of course Arnold and his parents didn't show up. They were probably in the reeds somewhere, still asleep. "Just like Arnold to be unreliable," Mitzi said, puffing away on a cigaret. "That bird is too much."

We were sitting on the little beach, watching the sunrise. "I'll send you pictures of him," I said. "When he's grown."

Mitzi smiled. "If you've seen one swan, you've seen them all."

It was supposed to be a joke, but neither of us laughed.

I had her present in my knapsack, but I didn't know when to give it to her. It had to be the right moment. "They say that New Mexico is a terrific place for photographers," I said. "The light and everything."

Mitzi blew a smoke ring and gazed out over the pond. "Yeah, I'm really looking forward to it. I mean, hell, Woodruff, you know how I love wild places, and New Mexico is extremely wild. I'll send you pictures of prairie dogs and rattlers."

"Don't get too western, or I won't recognize you when I come out to visit."

She looked away from me. "Right."

"I'm coming, you know. As soon as I can save the plane fare."

"Sure. I know."

I had wrapped her present in silver paper, and I wanted her to have it, but I still couldn't find the right moment. "Where's that goddam swan?" she said. "I wanted to take his picture."

I opened my knapsack and took out her present. Actually, there were three presents—the camera, the zoom lens, and the camera bag. "These are for you."

Mitzi looked at me suspiciously. "How come?"

"Because you're going away."

She opened the packages, first the camera, then the lens and the camera bag. And I saw that her mouth was twitching, like it always does when she is upset. "What the hell did you do?" she said. "You must be crazy."

"It's a going-away present, and a birthday present too. Your birthday is in November."

"You must have won another ice-cream contest."

"Do you like it?"

"Well, sure. But I can't accept . . ."

"Yes, you can," I said. "Because it's from me."

She was already mounting the zoom lens onto the camera body, and I could tell that she was excited. "Fantastic," she kept saying. "Fantastic."

We fooled around with the camera for a while, reading the literature that came with it—and shooting some film, as a trial run—but we both knew that the time was coming to say good-bye. Mitzi still had a lot of packing to do. "I have something to give you too," she said. "But it didn't cost any money."

"That's OK."

She handed me a small white envelope. "It's something I've carried around in my wallet for years. I clipped it out of a magazine."

I started to open the envelope. "No," she said. "Read it after I'm gone."

She rose to her feet and gave me a crooked grin. "It's been nice knowing you, kid. Take care of yourself."

"I'll be in Santa Fe before you know it."

"Right. I'll buy you a cowboy hat. And listen, I want to say two things . . . First, that you should call that brother of yours and make up with him. And second, that Crazy Vanilla was actually a very good name. I was just kidding you about it, you know. It was good."

I wanted to put my arms around her and hold her, and I think she wanted to hold me too. But instead, I just kissed her on the cheek, very quickly. The kind of kiss you would give to a relative. "So long, Mitzi."

She had packed up her new camera gear and was putting it into her bike basket. And though the corner of her mouth was still twitching, she tried to smile. "So long, Woodruff. See you around."

TWENTY-FOUR

I got up at five-thirty the next morning and rode my bike into town. I wanted to see the Gerrards leave—because I knew if I could just see them go, I would believe it and try to put the whole thing behind me. It's possible that this was a masochistic thing to do. I don't know. But I had to see them take off.

Sag Harbor always looks beautiful on Sunday mornings because it is so empty, and because the sun rises right over the wharf, where the big yachts are docked. All you are liable to see, on a Sunday, are a few dogs trotting up the street and sea gulls sitting on the railings of the bridge. At six o'clock the bells from the Catholic church begin to ring for early mass, and—considering the tourist trade in this place—Sunday morning is definitely the best time. Today was no exception. It was quiet and beautiful, and I saw the Gerrards right away, in front of Mustard Seed. They were packing the last of their possessions into Morton's van.

I parked my bike at a distance and watched. Mrs. Gerrard and Morton looked sleepy, but not Mitzi. She was directing the whole operation like some kind of stage manager, deciding where the dog would sit, and where the two kittens would go. (She had built them a big cage for the trip.) Morton's van was very large, but it was packed to the gills with their things. "Come on, Morton!" Mitzi was saying. "Let's move those suitcases over there. Then we'll have room for the kitchen stuff."

I stared hard at Mitzi, who was wearing her faded jeans and an old shirt, and whose hair, as usual, was standing straight on end. Stared at her so I would never forget her, and then the three of them were getting into the van. Mitzi looked at the town of Sag Harbor for a moment—at the wharf and the sunrise, and the main street—and then she got into the front seat, between her mother and Morton. In a second, they were gone.

I rode my bike back over the bridge, and though I hadn't intended to go to the pond, that's where I wound up. And wouldn't you know it, Arnold and his parents were there, sailing back and forth in the early light. Arnold looked huge. "Where were you *yesterday*?" I said to him. "Mitzi wanted to photograph you, for God's sake."

And then I started to cry.

I cried for a long time, and when I had finished crying I knew that Mitzi Gerrard was gone and that I would never see her again. I would never get to New Mexico, and we had both known it all along. But the worst part was that I hadn't told her that I loved her. You wait all your life to love someone, and then you can't even tell them about it. Can't even tell the simple truth.

I wiped my eyes and took out the envelope Mitzi had given me. And I opened it with great care, because I couldn't imagine what would be inside. But it was only a very wrinkled magazine clipping, a quotation from someone named Henry Beston. I had never heard of him.

We need another and a wiser and perhaps a more mystical concept of animals. Remote from universal nature, and living by complicated artifice, man in civilization surveys the creature through the glass of his knowledge and sees thereby a feather magnified and the whole image in distortion. We patronize them for their incompleteness, for their tragic fate of having taken form so far below ourselves. And therein we err, and greatly err. For the animal shall not be measured by man. In a world older and more complete than ours they move finished and complete, gifted with extensions of the senses we have lost or never attained, living by voices we shall never hear. They are not brethren, they are not underlings; they are other nations, caught with ourselves in the net of life and time, fellow prisoners of the splendour and travail of the earth.

TWENTY-FIVE

It's January now, and all the ponds in The Hamptons are frozen. The swans sit on them like statues, hungry and thin, and I spend a lot of time going around with bags of bread feeding everybody. Arnold and his parents have disappeared, flown off to a better place, perhaps, and after her first brood was hatched I never saw Zeppo again. Which is the way it goes, I guess. Nature.

In some ways, very little has changed for me. I mean, I still don't have many friends and still like birds better than people. And I still get up early every morning, and take my camera and head for the woods or the beach. But in other ways, everything has changed because of Mitzi Gerrard.

The way I see life and people, and probably the way I see myself. Because to tell you the truth, I'm not such a bad person. I've been taking Mother to AA meetings these days—open meetings, where anyone can attend—and while she hasn't committed herself to the program yet, at least she's willing to listen.

The thing about Mitzi is, we never wrote—never corresponded. After she left I composed dozens of letters to her, but never mailed them. Don't ask me why.

I think about Mitzi, and then I look into the future and see her and her camera in East Africa. I see her striding through the bush, stalking lions, with her gear slung over her shoulder and her eyes very determined. She still smokes like a chimney, but she is mature now and totally self-reliant. In my fantasy she has become famous, and her photos appear in *Life* and the *National Geographic.* She never got married, and her friends are few and far between. But she has done what she wanted to do in life—just like I will—and that's all that matters. We all have a destiny to follow, though most of us don't know it, and I think my destiny is going to be great.

One more thing. I phoned Cameron that Sunday, the day that I read Mitzi's magazine quote down by the pond. He had heard of Henry Beston.

OTHER PAPERBACK ORIGINALS

Bad Apple Larry Bograd
Breaktime Aidan Chambers
Children of the Dust Louise Lawrence
The Damned Linda Hoy
Dance on my Grave Aidan Chambers
Dear Comrade Frances Thomas
The Girl with a Voice Peggy Woodford
Harry and Hortense at Hormone High Paul Zindel
Hollywood Dream Machine Bonnie Zindel
If It Weren't for Sebastian . . . Jean Ure
I Love You, Stupid! Harry Mazer
Love Me, Love Rome Peggy Woodford
Misfits Peggy Woodford (Compiler)
Moonwind Louise Lawrence
My Darling Villain Lynne Reid Banks
Now I Know Aidan Chambers
One Green Leaf Jean Ure
The Other Side of the Fence Jean Ure
Out of Time (Stories of the Future) Aidan Chambers (Compiler)
An Overpraised Season Charlotte Zolotow (Compiler)
Over the Moon Elissa Haden Guest
Pictures of Adam Myron Levoy
Please Don't Go Peggy Woodford
A Proper Little Nooryeff Jean Ure
A Quiver of Ghosts Aidan Chambers (Compiler)
Rainbows of the Gutter Rukshana Smith
See You Tomorrow Peggy Woodford
Skindeep Toeckey Jones
A Sporting Chance Aidan Chambers (Compiler)
Sumitra's Story Rukshana Smith
Tunes for a Small Harmonica Barbara Wersba
The Warriors of Taan Louise Lawrence
Year King Penelope Farmer
Your Friend, Rebecca Linda Hoy
You Win Some, You Lose Some Jean Ure
Zak Frances Thomas